THEIRS

A DARK ODYSSEY NOVEL

KHARDINE GRAY

FAITH SUMMERS

Theirs

A Dark Odyssey Novella

USA Today Bestselling Author
Khardine Gray
writing as
Faith Summers

DARK ROMANCE NOTE

AUTHOR NOTE

Please note Faith Summers is the Dark romance pen name of USA Today Bestselling Author Khardine Gray

THEY NEEDED ME. AND I NEEDED THEM TOO...

I'm broken again.

This time my life is in danger.

Desperation has sent me running right back through the doors of the Dark Odyssey.

For those with money, the club is the Billionaire's Playground.

The heathens haven of dark fantasy.

But for those like me, it's the gateway to sell your soul when you have nothing left to give.

After my deceitful ex-husband left me in a mountain of debt, working at the club was my only option.

Then I met them—Cristiano, Knox, and Levi.

The ruthless leader, the vicious protector, and the daring rebel.

They gave me a way out of the devil's contract—

All I have to do is become Cristiano's wife so he can inherit his empire and all my problems will disappear.

Knox and Levi are the added bonus.

Perfection.

Except this isn't a fairy tale.
If our secret arrangement is discovered it's game over.

1

MEGAN

I never thought I'd become a whore again.

I loathe that word—w*hore*. It's a cruel, vile thing to christen myself, but what else can I say I am if I'm about to sell my body?

It doesn't matter which color I paint what I'm about to do, the truth is the truth, and nothing can change that.

Even if becoming a whore is my only chance of saving myself, this is the second time I've had to sell my soul to the dark side.

At twenty-seven years old, with a degree in Psychology under my belt, I honestly thought my life would be different now.

I also never expected to become a widow at such a young age or for my dead husband to be a fraud who screwed me over in every way possible when I inherited the half-million-dollar debt he left in my name.

I can't even tell anyone the truth about him or the debt because I'm dead if I do.

I was warned not to trust him. I just never listened. Love

blindsided me and made me the perfect pawn for Hunter's game of lies.

Hunter Reid was my high school sweetheart and, for me, the one who got away. I wanted to believe he was the one good thing from my past that found its way back to me. But he wasn't.

That's why I'm here tonight on the doorstep of The Dark Odyssey, the infamous sex club those with money as old as dirt call the billionaires' playground.

Owned by the Giordanos—an Italian mafia family—it's nestled in the heart of one of Chicago's busiest streets.

Tonight I'm going back through their doors as a returning staff member. After a two-year absence, I'll resume my role as a *special* waitress.

Special, meaning one of the girls who you can book for anything. Literally *anything.*

I make my way up the sweeping marble steps to the club's doors and observe tonight's patrons under the moonlit sky.

The women are all dressed in sexy lingerie, while the men wear dress shirts and suits. Everyone has on the Venetian masquerade masks for the club's customary party. These parties are held every night and are part of the dark fantasy of being here.

I make my way into the foyer and spot Mimi Giordano talking to one of the receptionists at the concierge desk. Mimi is married to Salvatore Giordano, one of the club owners. She takes care of the girls who work here.

She smiles when she sees me, and I do the same.

When I reach her, she gives me a hug that feels as sympathetic as her voice did when I called her the other day to ask for my old job back. I told her my husband had died and sounded like the grieving wife I played to everyone else.

The thing is, it's not an act. I'm grieving for so many things, just not the reasons everyone believes.

"It's great to see you." Mimi's smile brightens, and her long blond curls bounce as she nods.

"You too."

"Come, let's go talk for a little while." She gestures to the elevator.

"Thanks, I'd like that." I'm eager for the night to be over but not eager to start. With the contract I've signed, I could likely end up being some rich bastard's sex toy. While that's where the money is, and would have appealed to me in my younger days, I'm not that girl anymore.

This version of myself was en route to having a respectable career as a therapist. Now I don't know when I'll be able to get back to that.

We go into the elevator and get off on the third floor. Mimi takes me into her office, where she motions for me to sit on the white leather sofa by the floor-to-ceiling glass walls. It has a fabulous view of the Chicago skyline lit up by the city lights. I've always admired the view whenever I've been here.

She sits opposite me and sighs heavily, brushing her hair over her shoulders.

"I just wanted to talk to you properly before you start," she begins. "How are you doing?"

"I'm... getting there." My answer feels like more lies spewing from my mouth, but I don't want her to think I can't do the job. They have a policy here about being part of the fantasy. So you have to put on a show, regardless of how you feel.

"I'm truly sorry about Hunter."

"Thanks."

"It was such a horrible accident."

Accident? No, Mimi, it wasn't an accident.

Sure, that's what it looked like when it made the evening news, but Hunter's death was no accident.

He was found in his car in the woods by the Chicago River. The car, along with his body, was torched. The only thing the coroner could use to identify him was his dental records. What I buried a month ago was his charred skeleton.

"I know I'm your boss, and we haven't seen each other in years, but please let me know if you need to talk."

"I will." The most important thing I've learned from my extensive studies on treatment therapies is talking helps. Talking takes the edge off our worries even when we want to keep our feelings locked away from the world. But not if it could get you killed. Like it would in my case.

"I know how hard things must have been losing your husband like that. I can't imagine what you must be going through." Her voice deepens with emotion, and she presses a hand to her heart.

"It's been awful." *Another half-truth.*

When I first learned of Hunter's death, my world ended. At the time, we'd only been married for two weeks. Then not even a full day after the news broke, it became clear that one of the many enemies I didn't know about must have killed him. I travel in enough circles to know that burning a person up is the best way to cover what really happened.

I wish I could say that to Mimi, but then she'd have questions I can't or mustn't answer. Like why am I not looking for Hunter's killers, or how did I fall so quickly out of love with him.

And why don't I care? Or maybe she'd skip all that and

jump to the part where she'd ask why I think it's appropriate to work in a sex club barely six weeks after I got married and buried my husband.

None of it is right. But I'm a woman who was given two choices. Become a sex worker on my own terms to clear the debt or do it under forced conditions where I'd belong to Hunter's debtors forever.

Once again, I'm alone with no friends, no family, and no one I can trust enough to turn to. So this is the way forward.

I lift my chin and pull in a measured breath to steady my mind and the ache in my heart. "Thank you for allowing me to come back here."

"You know you always have a job at the Dark Odyssey."

"I appreciate that." I do, even if I'm praying I'll never have to work here again after this. As much as I have a wild side which would enjoy coming here for fun with my man—*if I ever have one of those again*—I'm not sure I'd want to come back ever again. People don't tend to want to have fun in the places where they lost their souls.

Sympathy brims in Mimi's eyes. She's been working here since the club opened its doors over a decade ago. She knows what desperate looks like and what would push a girl to sign her body up for anything.

"I've arranged for you to take care of the VIP list," she says.

That's perfect, and I'm sure it will help me massively. VIP clients often pay you to be exclusive to them. I got lucky like that last time and made enough to put myself through college.

"Thanks so much." At least tonight is starting out promising.

"No worries. Tonight you have a group of three guys who are all best friends."

That translates to guys who like group sex. I've had three-somes here before. Adding one more guy to the mix will be different for me.

"They're here for a business meeting, so you might have a short night."

"That's fine." Short is great, but realistically, it doesn't matter. What's important is the end goal. So I need to push aside my reservations and embrace whatever I need to do to get my life back.

"Are you ready?"

"I am."

"Great, I'll take you to the dressing room first, then we can go upstairs and meet the guys."

"Thanks."

When we get to the dressing room, my clothes are already laid out for me.

There's a sheer black negligee made from material so thin it's completely see-through. My light pink nipples are visible against the fabric when I put it on. That's the idea though. Clothes like these are just a tease for the men.

At least the matching thong has a thicker bit of fabric covering my mound—*just barely.*

I'm comfortable with my body, and like most girls here, I'm okay to go topless, but I don't like showing more until I get intimate with someone.

Once my hair and makeup are done, I look like I could fit right in with the ladies at the Moulin Rouge. Mimi then ushers me through the door to the left, which goes right into the club. Instantly I'm immersed in flashing strobe lights and the wild club mix music cocooned in the beautiful Venetian-style hall with its high gold ceiling and classy European décor.

I've been to Venice and Rome, so I'm confident in endorsing the design this hall attempts to replicate.

The sea of partygoers on the dancefloor below are having fun, but the first thing anybody notices when they walk in is the people having sex.

Tonight it looks like everyone is doing it.

There are people having sex in the Arabian-style cubicles on the sidelines of the dance floor, people having sex in the sofa areas by the bar, and people having sex against the walls.

I consider myself sexually adventurous. During my time here, I've gotten up to all sorts of debauchery, but it's still shocking for me to see everyone like this out in the open.

People like Mimi don't flicker an eyelid because being here all the time makes public sex feel commonplace. People like me gawk the way I am now at the acrobatic couple fucking on the ariel hoop in the ceiling as they sail past us.

I've seen that before, but it still throws me. The same as watching the threesome in the exhibitionist box at the far corner of the room.

This is what you call a dark fantasy. In the Dark Odyssey, sex is very much an art as dancing, singing, or painting because the owners think it's an expression of your inner desires.

We branch off the balcony and walk through the fantasy maze where more couples blend in with the shadows against the wall. I'm then taken to the VIP lounge.

I gear myself up to meet *the guys*. But as Mimi opens the

door to the first room, I realize nothing could prepare me for the sight of the three drop-dead gorgeous Italian men inside.

Dressed in full black and standing next to the table with the decanter and wine, they look like they're posing for a GQ Magazine photoshoot.

I'm certainly not prepared for the raw heat spiking my nerves or for the deliciously sexy sight of them to wipe my brain clean of everything.

When the guy with the bright blue eyes looks at me with mischief lurking in his gaze, and the other two exchange curious glances that hold the same air of sexiness, I know I'm going to have one very interesting night.

2

MEGAN

"Hi," I say when Mimi leaves us. "I'm Megan."

"Pretty name for a pretty face," says Mr. Blue Eyes. The other two both have autumn brown eyes.

"Thank you."

"I'm Cristiano, and this is Levi and Knox." He points to the other two guys, respectively.

Levi is taller than Knox. Judging from the sculpt of his body, he looks like he's lived in a gym all his life. Knox and Cristiano, on the other hand, look like they've served in the marines. They are each so ridiculously gorgeous I'm having a hard time looking away from them.

"Hello." I give them each a smile.

"Hello, Goddess." Levi winks at me.

"Buona serata." Knox dips his head and makes a point of staring at my breasts. He has gorgeous, kissable lips. The kind you could sink into and kiss forever.

"Do you speak Italian?" Cristiano asks, drawing my attention back to him. His gaze drops from my face and goes straight to my pussy.

The scandalous look he gives me evokes an immediate reaction from my body. It takes me by surprise because moisture is gathering between my thighs as if I've been starved for sex for years.

I almost forget what he asked me until his gaze flicks back up to mine, and he arches a stern brow.

Italian. Do I speak it? Not a damn bit which is terrible considering I've worked with Italians for years.

"No. I wish I did."

"That's no problem for us." Knox states.

"Come and sit with us." Levi waves me over.

When I go to them, we sit on the leather sofa.

Knox and Levi sit on either side of me while Cristiano lowers to the chair in front. I'm completely blocked in, and I think that was by design.

"Why don't you tell us about yourself, Megan," Cristiano says, and I feel like I'm in an interview. I guess it is, and he's trying to vet me to see what he wants to do with me.

What the hell do I tell him? I didn't plan for this part. Most clients of the past just wanted to fuck me. They didn't care about knowing me.

"I'm twenty-seven. I've worked here on and off for a couple of years."

At the mention of my years of service, Cristiano glances at Knox, and the corners of his lips tip into a half smile unleashing sinful dimples.

He inclines his head to the side, and a lock of hair falls over his eye like curtains at a window. It makes me think of how people say our eyes are windows to our souls.

When I stare back at him and look deep into his eyes, I see nothing but the Prussian blue color and lust. There's nothing else that might give away who he is.

"Can we assume that means you're used to groups?"

"Yes." I look at each of them and try to figure out their dynamics. I guess Cristiano is the leader of the pack because there's an air of dominance about him. Knox has the same presence but looks like he follows Cristiano's command. Levi looks like the silent rebel who throws you off kilter when you least expect it.

"Groups of how many?" Knox asks.

My cheeks flush. This is a different version of asking me how many men I've slept with. This question is how many at the same time.

"Three, with me included."

"We're a little different." Cristiano smiles, and at that moment, a flicker of something in his eyes gives me a glimpse of what I think is danger.

It's the same vibe I usually sense from mafia men.

Is that what they are? It wouldn't be impossible given the number of men from the Sicilian mafia who frequent the club due to the connections with the owners.

"How so?"

"We all like attention. We like giving and receiving it in specific ways."

"Together?" I'm curious because they all seem straight.

"No. We don't touch, ever. We just like to share. We share everything, including attention, so we know how to divide that. It's nice when our women can do the same, and of course, we make sure she's well taken care of."

My mouth waters when I think of how they would do that for me.

"I'm sure I can do what you need." I look at each of them.

Knox and Levi exchange smiles, but Cristiano doesn't take his eyes off me.

"Is there something you'd like me to start with?" I always ask that question to kick start the fantasy.

"Yes." Cristiano looks away from me, then says something to Knox and Levi in Italian.

Of course, I don't know what he's saying, but God, his accent. Wow, it's so sexy.

His eyes dart back to mine, and he straightens, tucking his hair behind his ear. "We want to start with tasting you."

That mouthwatering feeling comes back to assault me. "Tasting me?"

"Yes." He gives me a wicked grin.

"I thought this evening was about me pleasing you." I keep my voice steady, hoping I won't show how much I'd love for them to taste me.

"It is." He grins, allowing his eyes to fall up and down my body. "Show her what I mean, boys."

"Come here, Goddess." Knox crooks his finger toward me, and I move to him as if attached to strings.

He moves to me too, placing those kissable lips on mine. The moment our lips touch, the raw fire of arousal blazes within my body and I savor the spellbinding effect pulsing through me.

I'm entirely absorbed, so when warm fingers flutter down my arm, I assume it's him. It's not until another set of lips press against the left side of my neck that I realize it has to be Levi. His touch does something to me that feels like it's soothing me from the inside out.

More fiery kisses are pressed along my neck while Knox kisses my lips. Then Levi's fingers drop to my breast and he rubs my nipple beneath the silky fabric of my negligée. He catches my nipple between his fingers and tweaks it, then massages my breast. The pleasure of his gentle touch blends with the arousal coiling through me and my body bows. Wetness gushes from my pussy, and I lose control of my mind.

When Knox moves away from my lips and trails kisses down the side of my neck, instinct turns me to Levi, and we kiss. It's as if the three of us rehearsed this; it feels so natural.

Kissing Levi is just as delicious as kissing Knox. When he cups my other breast and does the same thing Levi is doing, my body tightens with pleasure, leaving me breathless, mindless, senseless.

As the guys continue pleasuring me, I'm suddenly aware Cristiano is just watching us.

When I look at him, I take note of the fascination on his face and realize he likes watching. Quickly, I guess he must be a voyeur.

Levi draws my attention back to him with a kiss, and he and Knox continue fondling me.

Just as I manage to control myself so I can enjoy them, they stop everything, leaving me panting like I've been running for days.

My cheeks flush when I look at Cristiano and notice the hungry predatory expression on his handsome face.

"This needs to come off." He lifts the hem of my negligee and I raise my arms so he can pull it over my head, exposing my naked breasts. Then in perfect synchronicity switches places with Levi, who positions between my legs. "It's my turn to taste you."

My already sensitive nipples harden when Cristiano lowers to suck them. He moves from one breast to the other, sending streaks of scorching pleasure rushing straight to my core. I come undone, moaning and pushing against the soft leather of the sofa to keep myself from falling off the face of reality.

At the sound of my elation, he ceases his wild assault on my breasts and crushes his mouth to mine.

I could have guessed that kissing this man would sweep me out of this world. Now I know it, and I allow his dominance to possess me.

Moments later, Knox resumes sucking my breast while Levi rolls my thong down my legs. When he parts my thighs wider, he buries his face in my pussy so he can push his tongue into my passage. And oh God, my orgasm rises like a relentless tidal wave.

At the touch of all three men, my body comes alive in a way I can't describe with words, and I come. I come so hard that my body shudders as if I've been caught up in the depths of an earthquake.

Moments pass with us like this—me naked kissing Cristiano while he plays with my right breast, Knox sucking my left, and Levi eating out my pussy.

Just as I climb down from the high, Knox and Levi switch places sending me right back to the pinnacle of pleasure. Knox laps at my clit as if I'm some rare exotic meal and I arch into the wild sensation washing over me.

I feel like I'm going to go insane when my jaw is turned to the left so I can kiss Levi while Cristiano sucks my breast. The pleasure is too much, yet I can't get enough of it.

I come again, and the guys switch out once more. I'm so lost I don't even know who I'm kissing and who's doing what. I just know I feel amazing and I don't want them to stop tasting me.

They feast on me. All of them, tasting every inch of my body from head to toe.

Lips move away from mine, and I see I was kissing Knox. He and Levi go to my breasts while Cristiano swirls his tongue over my pussy lips. He tugs on my clit, and I come once more, but this time I come for him, and I scream.

The dominance in his touch tells me we're not finished until he's had the final taste.

My breathing calms and my awareness returns, clearing the sexual haze.

Cristiano's devastating smile freezes me in place as he stands. Knox and Levi rise too when he says something in Italian.

Cristiano is talking to them but doesn't take his eyes off me. I wish I knew what he was saying.

I know I'm about to find out when Cristiano lowers and hovers a few inches away from my lips.

"We have to go now, but we've decided we like you. *I* like you, and we want to see you again." Everything he says is with emphasis.

I blink several times. "You want to see me again?"

"Yes, Goddess. I'll leave instructions for you on where to meet us tomorrow. Then you get to taste us. Understand?"

"Yes."

"Good girl. You can go home now."

He straightens and I watch the three of them leave.

It's not until the door closes behind them that I release the breath I'm holding.

I knew to expect anything from tonight, but I never thought I'd be left feeling like I'd been caught in the eye of a storm with my brain scrambled and my body on fire.

I definitely never thought I'd be eager to come back tomorrow so I could get my chance to taste the three gorgeous men who took me out of reality.

It hasn't escaped me that they made tonight about me.

Not them.

3

CRISTIANO

The woman was fucking magic.

The image of her decadent body with her silky black hair, bright brown eyes, and sultry red lips floats into my mind.

Women like Megan make the Dark Odyssey what it is for me.

The Dark Odyssey is one of the first places the guys and I visit when we're in Chicago. We all love the escapism and the craziness the club owners do to cater to men like us with dark tastes.

My only regret about last night was not having the time to truly do all I wanted to do to the beautiful goddess.

If we didn't have to meet with Vincent Giordano about his new business venture in Italy, we would have had all sorts of sinful fun with Megan. I would have at the very least had my dick sliding between those pillowy lips of her pretty mouth.

To relieve the ache in my dick, I found myself jerking off in my shower when I returned to my fortress of a home. I haven't had to do that in a long time because I always get what I want, whenever and wherever I want.

I'm Cristiano Rivera, and I've always lived by the strength and power of my name. Last night was one of those times when I had to put business first.

My family's business is in property development. We have a long-standing business relationship with the Giordanos. Vincent is the don of the family. His brothers and cousins own the Dark Odyssey.

As a man on his way to taking over his family business, I needed to look professional last night in front of Rivera Developments' most important client.

I couldn't look like the playboy or the rebel. There's a time for that. It wasn't last night, and it's not now either.

I tamp down my lust as I walk into the meeting room and my gaze settles on my grandfather sitting at the head of the long mahogany table. Lorenzo, his consigliere—advisor and second in command, is seated to his right. The fucker is also the prick who would love to have my legacy.

The last time we met, he tried to persuade my grandfather to pull me off the European projects. He thought I was going to fuck things up because I pissed off one of the investors. I proved the asshole wrong by getting a better investment and making a billion dollars on top as profit.

So the smug go-fuck-yourself smile I'm giving him is well deserved, and he knows it. That's why he's finding it hard to look me in the eye.

Motherfucker. When I take over, I'm kicking his ass out. I don't care how long he's worked for my family or how valuable he is. He's gone. A leader can't afford to have trust issues or any kind of contention with their subordinates. It weakens the structure of any business.

My great, great grandfather might have built this company, but my men and I took it to places no one ever envisaged. We've spent the last six years taking care of all the projects in Europe, the US, and the Caribbean. We turned the company into a different kind of legacy for the future.

"Buongiorno." I dip my head toward Grandfather first, then Lorenzo, just to be respectful in my grandfather's presence.

"Buongiorno, my boy." The rust in Grandfather's voice is from too many years of smoking but is more pronounced today. "It's good to see you."

"You too."

Lorenzo doesn't say anything to me. Instead, he tries to mask the put-out expression on his face with a fake as fuck smile I can see straight through. It's hard to believe he was ever my father's best friend. This man absolutely loathes the fact that I live and breathe.

Grandfather looks me over the way a parent would when they haven't seen their child in a long time. As it's been six months since we last saw each other, I make my way over to him and air kiss his cheeks. He, however, being the fatherly figure he is, pulls me in for a hug.

Affection like this doesn't come easy for a man like him. He's the ruthless mafia boss when he needs to be, but he values family.

Five years ago, when my father died, Grandfather became my everything. I, in turn, became more like a son to him.

I take the seat to his left, keeping my gaze on Lorenzo.

"I heard last night went extremely well," Grandfather says with pride.

When I think of last night, Megan enters my mind again.

I think of the good time I had with her and the delicious taste of her pussy.

He's not talking about that though. My grandfather must have gotten a good report from Vincent.

"I'm glad to hear that."

"Another job well done."

"Thank you. You know I aim to please."

"I do, and it makes me proud." He nods and brings his gnarled hands together.

"I'm happy to hear you say that." I cut Lorenzo a glance, noting how quiet he is. It's unusual, but since I hate the sound of his voice, his silence is fine by me.

"I'm sure you are. Anyway, I know we both have a busy day, so I'll cut to the chase and get on to the matter of transferring the empire to you."

"I'll take that as my cue to leave." Lorenzo pushes to his feet and adjusts his jacket. When he smiles, I take that as a sign he's privy to some shit about handing over the business I don't know. "I'll catch up with you both later."

"Okay." Grandfather glances at him then looks back at me when Lorenzo goes through the door. "I'm sure you've been eager to talk about this since I mentioned it."

"I have." I've been waiting for this moment since he declared his plans

six months ago. As my grandfather's eldest male heir, the business is supposed to pass to me when he retires.

Back then, he wanted me to do certain things which I've done and more than proven myself. Knox and Levi have too. They are my right-hand men and will be my capos when I take the lead. We've always worked together and have been friends since birth because their families worked for Rivera Developments.

When I take over, I want them to be equal business partners because they've earned it.

"There are a few things I still need you to do," Grandfather declares.

My nerves spike. "Like what?"

He frowns, deepening the creases already etched on his forehead. "When my grandfather set up this company, it was very important to him to have a legacy that would carry the family name forever. I need to respect that."

"I respect that too." I already sense where this conversation is going—because we've had it before. It's the whole marriage thing. He's wanted me to get married since I was eighteen. I've successfully dodged his attempts to get me hitched for the last eleven years.

"I know you respect it, but not the way I do. You've been engaged to your Evelina for over a year, and I still haven't met her."

My chest tightens at the mention of Evelina—a.k.a my biggest tactic to

escape his last attempt at an arranged marriage.

She also doesn't exist.

Every time my grandfather talks about her, I wonder how the fuck I'm going to get myself around the situation. I've only managed to get away with making him believe she exists because I'm constantly traveling and he hardly sees me. I also believe I sold him the idea because he thinks I fell in love like he did with my grandmother.

"Grandfather, you know she travels a lot. Just like me." I told him my dear Evelina works with charities so is often working in some country doing her humanitarian projects.

"And what about the wedding?" His eyes bore into me. "When will that be?"

"We're talking about it."

"You said that six months ago. If this continues, you'll be perpetually engaged and never get married."

That's the fucking idea. I was going to break up with my made-up girlfriend after I got the business. At that point, I'd be in charge with my own rules.

I appreciate he wants me settled down and wants to impart his wisdom on me, but marriage is a minor detail neither of us needs to worry about. Definitely not when the company is doing so well.

"Grandfather, you don't have to worry about Evelina and me. And you don't have to worry about the company either." I rivet my gaze to his fading blue eyes, instilling the subtle change of subject. "You know I'm capable. The guys and I have done wonders as a team. The Giordanos and all our high-profile clientele are impressed with us. The empire is in safe hands. There's *nothing* to worry about. All you can expect from us is more success, wealth, and power."

"My dear boy, you're talking about everything besides the one thing I value the most."

Family. I bite down hard on my back teeth and try to tamp down my annoyance. The subject of family shouldn't be annoying, but it is when he brings it up with business.

"Family is our legacy." His face becomes softer, his eyes less guarded and harsh. "If I pass the empire to you. I need to know it will continue with you."

I hate the way he said *if.* I want to ask him what the fuck he means by it, but I hold my tongue and contemplate other ways of clarifying.

"What do you want me to do?" I try to keep my tone even.

"Get married. That is the last thing I want you to do before I sign over the business to you."

What the fuck? I couldn't have heard him right. I look at him as if he's just hit me with a fifty-ton truck.

"Grandfather, you're not serious." He can't fucking be, and if he is, then this can't be happening. Not after all my hard work.

"I'm serious as fuck, boy." He raises his chin. "I want to meet your fiancée when I get back from New Orleans, and I want to see you marry her in the same church your father married your mother. If you can't do that, then you have a problem."

Fuck me and my fucking lies.

"This isn't fair by any means."

"Maybe not, but this is the way I've chosen. Especially since I've found another way of securing the Rivera legacy."

Everything inside me goes numb. "What do you mean?"

"Your cousin Simona turns nineteen in a few months. She will take your place if you don't get married."

I stare back at him with my eyes wide, my jaw clamped, my heart doubling over.

Simona would be the next in line to own the business if I died or if there were some reason for my grandfather to change the rules.

"You're changing the rules—"

"Lorenzo has agreed to marry her."

"Lorenzo has agreed to do *what?*"

"You heard me."

"Lorenzo is nearly the same fucking age as you." Lorenzo just turned seventy-five.

"It doesn't matter. He's a suitable candidate."

I shake my head in disgust even though I can see what he means. Lorenzo is only suitable because his wife died several years ago, leaving him with three daughters who were married before I was of age. I just can't believe this is the way my grandfather has found to bend me to his will.

"So despite all I've done, you're going to force me to get married or lose everything?"

"I'm not forcing you to do anything, but if you want the business, I need a wedding. When you told me you were engaged, I turned Mary away. She would have made a good wife for you. She and her husband are expecting their first child now. That could have been you. Not to mention the amazing business relationship we turned away by rejecting the marriage contract."

Mary is the daughter of one of our business partners who own an oil refinery. Our marriage would have been a good business deal, but I didn't want to get married then, and I still don't want to.

Men like me don't get married. Men like me love fucking around at sex clubs like the Dark Odyssey with women like Megan, and more importantly, love fucking the same woman with his best friends.

"I don't think marriage should have any bearing on the company transfer."

"That is where you and I differ, Cristiano. Right now, all you are is a phenomenal employee. But I need the whole package. We are one of the oldest families in Chicago from the alliance that formed in Sicily over a hundred years ago. How will it look if you have no wife, no heirs, no family of your own? That is not what I want. That wasn't what your father wanted either."

At the mention of my father, my stomach clenches. He knows I would have done anything for my old man. Father spent his last days passing on all his knowledge to me. Even at his lowest points, when it was clear his heart was giving out, I knew his determination for me to do well in life kept it beating longer than it should have. My father showed the same determination to get me clean when I nearly lost myself to hardcore drugs.

Grandfather clears his throat. "I'm giving you three months to organize a wedding with your Evelina. If it doesn't happen by then, I'm going forward with my plans for Lorenzo and Simona. These are my terms." He opens the document folder in front of him and slides a sheet of paper over to me.

The fucking thing actually looks like the terms and conditions document we draw up for our contracts. But this is about my marriage. The first page is covered with conditions from numbers one to twenty. My gaze rivets to the first because it's the one that hits me like a punch to my gut.

It says:

All assets belonging to Rivera Developments will be transferred for a probationary period after your marriage. In order for full transfer to take place, the marriage will need to last for a minimum of three years. After such time full transfer will be awarded.

"Everything in this document is designed to guide you." Grandfather runs a finger over the top of the page. "I assure you this is all coming from a place of love."

I don't know how he thinks that makes sense. It doesn't. This is an assertion of his dominance over me. A big fuck you to everything the guys and I have done and a reminder of how things work—his way or no way.

"That's it? There's no compromise?" My eyes lock with his.

"No. There is none."

Which means if I don't think of a way to get what I want, I'm fucked.

There's no way I'm going to lose everything to Lorenzo.

So I have to find an Evelina.

A woman who will firstly marry me and second, stay married to me for three years.

Fuck.

4

MEGAN

"Holy fucking shit, it's real." I keep my eyes glued to my laptop screen, confirming the number of zeros I can see on my bank balance.

There's really ten thousand dollars in my account, and it came from

Cristiano Rivera.

Cristiano, as in Cristiano from last night, and Rivera, as in one of the biggest property developers in the US. When I saw his surname listed on the transaction, I looked him up and was completely blown away to find out who he is.

The Riveras also have strong mafia connections, which is no surprise. I suspected it from last night.

This is unreal. I can't believe he paid me so much for allowing him and his friends to play with me.

I'm beyond shocked. So shocked I'm afraid to look away from the screen in case the money disappears.

I woke to the notification on my phone that the money had been deposited. When I saw how much it was, I grabbed my laptop and logged into my account to check I hadn't gone crazy.

Initial payments are supposed to go through the club, but there are exceptions for special people. It's obvious Cristiano is one of them. He would need to be, to be allowed my bank details. That means he knows my full name too and might be aware I've been recently widowed.

It's possible. It's also possible he might not know because I didn't get the chance to use my married name. Everything to identify me is still in my maiden name, and thank God my name has been kept out of the media. But, when dealing with men like Cristiano, such things might be irrelevant. Men like him could find out pretty much everything about me by clicking a button.

It doesn't matter. I don't care if he knows I was married or that Hunter died. No one knows the fine print of what I'm left dealing with regarding Hunter's debtors and the shit.

When I see Cristiano tonight, I'll have nothing but gratitude for him. I'm not supposed to show how thankful I am because it messes with the fantasy, but I have to thank him.

This money means I'll be able to pay Hunter's asshole debtor, Bill Rodriguez, a little over twenty thousand dollars this month. I'll drop off the money I have later on my way to work and make another trip in a few weeks when I get paid from the club.

Bill came knocking on my door mere moments after the cops came to deliver the news of Hunter's death.

The last time I went to his office, I experienced that make-or-break moment that made me realize I had no choice but to go back to the Dark Odyssey.

After paying the asshole the thirty thousand dollars I had in the savings account Hunter didn't know about, I had a thousand dollars left to pay my rent. Bill wanted me to choose between giving him the money or sucking his dick.

When he forced me to my knees to shove his cock down my throat, I gave him the money. That was only two weeks ago.

After I spoke to Mimi and got my job back, I was able to make the agreement with Bill to pay back ten grand a month for the next two years.

Two years' salary from the club won't pay everything back, but it will get my foot through the door for opportunities like last night.

I've also deferred my training placement at UCLA with the hope that I can get back on track by the end of my penance.

Maybe then I'll be able to fix things with Paige too.

I met Paige Marchesi in my freshman year at Rutherford University. She was my very best friend and like a sister to me. Having come from a background of hardship similar to mine, she easily became the one person I shared all my secrets with.

The breakup of my six-year friendship with her was my biggest mistake.

She was right about Hunter, and I didn't want her to be.

We fell out last year after he proposed. Paige didn't trust him and saw the evil in him I couldn't see. No one was more against my relationship with him than her.

At the time, I thought she didn't want me to be happy, and I said some unforgivable things to her.

After Bill gave me the rude awakening about Hunter's dirty dealings, I contacted Gibbs, the private investigator I met through James, Paige's husband.

Gibbs is an unconventional P.I. used by a lot of people in

the criminal underground. James knew him through his mafia connections. He hired Gibbs to help me find my step-father, who disappeared after my mother died and took my inheritance. I always believed my stepfather had something to do with her death.

I was eighteen years old when she died and left with nothing but the clothes on my back. Gibbs never found my stepfather but was able to get evidence that showed he was still alive. It was way more than what the police found because it gave me a lead to continue my search whenever I get the money again.

Gibbs helped me again when he found out my dearly departed had stolen all my savings. A grand total of three hundred thousand dollars. That was everything I had to finish paying for grad school, put a deposit on a house, and also set up my own private practice when I qualified.

He found out Hunter used my money to pay for drugs, prostitutes, and splash out on luxury vacations for the wife and kids I never knew he had.

The motherfucking bastard was already married, and he had two kids under

five.

Months before Hunter proposed to me, Paige claimed she'd seen him with a woman and two small kids at Millennium Park. When she said he and the woman looked like a couple, we had the biggest argument ever. It turned out that the woman Paige described and the kids were the ones Gibbs showed me pictures of.

When Gibbs finished laying out all the dirty secrets, I didn't know what the fuck to do with myself. Of course, everything fell apart, including going back to L.A. to finish my training.

After finding out that my dead husband was a cheating, lying, thieving bastard, the worst thing was not having anyone to turn to for help.

Paige and James have been in Italy for the last eight months, so neither of them even knows Hunter is dead. Or maybe they do and think I deserve what I'm getting.

No... Paige isn't like that. No matter how badly our friendship ended, she wouldn't wish anything bad on me.

She would also hate that I had to go back to the club.

My life has been such a disaster, and I chased away the one good person who loved me.

Paige was possibly the only one who could have helped me now.

If I hadn't burned the bridge between us, Paige would have been the first person to come to my rescue when the shit hit the fan.

If I hadn't called her a selfish bitch and told her to stay away from me, I could have run to her after the threats were issued on my life. James would have kept me safe because that's the kind of man he is. He takes care of his wife and those important to her.

If I hadn't singlehandedly destroyed my friendship with Paige, I would still have a friend.

Some things can't be undone. But if I get out of this mess, the first thing I'll do is fix things with her.

I just have to survive first.

"Fucking hell." Bill's eyes nearly pop out of his head as he looks at the ten thousand dollar check I just handed him.

I roll my eyes when he holds it up to the light, checking it's real.

"How the fuck did you manage to get this?" His Columbian accent deepens. "It's a fuck of a lot of money for a woman who was broke weeks ago." His dark eagle eyes flick back to mine with raw scrutiny.

"That's none of your concern. I'm paying the debt, so there shouldn't be a problem."

"I just wouldn't want anything preventing you from continuing your payments."

Lies. He doesn't care about me that way. Judging from the sullen expression on his scar-riddled toad-like face, what he doesn't like is that I was able to pay such a huge amount. The motherfucker wants me to fail so I can become one of his sex slaves. Better yet, he wants me to be his fuck toy.

"I can assure you there won't be anything of the sort."

Bill places the check down on the desk, swipes a hairy hand through his balding head, then looks me up and down.

"Looks like you've been cashing in on your assets." He looks at my breasts and licks his lips.

My stomach churns when he flicks his tongue out. I hate this guy. He looks like old dried-up shit but has the kind of ego and confidence a better-looking man would have. Money can do that for you and make you believe any type of shit you make up in your reality.

Deciding to ignore his comment, I summon courage I don't feel. "I'll be back as soon as I have more money." Hopefully, I'll have another spell of luck like last night.

He laughs and brings his hands together. "You think you call the shots?"

"No, I'm just telling you I'll be back as soon as I have more money." *Never show fear, even when you're terrified.*

32

That's what Mom used to say, and I'm listening to the words engraved on my heart again. During this crazy time, her voice has been coming to me stronger than ever before. My mother was a strong, ambitious woman who had to fight hard to become the successful actress she was.

I might not have a career like she did, but I'm her through and through. I'm the kind of woman who will keep fighting even when I've been kicked down on the ground a million times, and there's nothing left for me to hold on to. So I won't show this man just how fucking scared I am of him.

"Alright, baby. You win today's round, but I'm still curious to know what those lips of yours will feel like around my dick." He laughs. "Or better yet, what it will feel like to fuck you. My men are just as curious as me."

"That's not going to happen." I swallow hard and try to keep the bile churning in my gut from spewing out.

"Never say never, Chica. People have to pay bills somehow. If I were you, I'd be grateful fucking is still an option."

No. It's not an option. Fucking him and his asshole men is not the same as being at the club. I'm not stupid. I know I'd never be free if I choose that way out.

I don't bother to answer. I just turn around and walk away, holding my breath until I'm back behind the steering wheel of my car.

I gaze at the shady as shit *office* I just came out of and shudder. It's at the back of a pawn shop which I know is a front for some sort of prostitution ring Bill is running. It's where I'll end up if I fail.

I should drive the hell away because it's eight o'clock at night, I'm in the rough part of town where there is always trouble, and there are all sorts of undesirable men standing by the walls watching me. But I'm looking and wondering how the fuck I ended up here.

How could this happen when I went through so much shit after Mom's death?

I want to pinch myself until I bleed so I can wake from this nightmare, but I know this is my hell.

The tears of the girl inside me want to come out. One slips down my cheek, and that's all the woman I need to be will allow.

One tear, one break, one moment of weakness. That's it.

I start the car up and head to the Dark Odyssey.

When I get there, I change into a negligée similar to what I wore last night and make my way up to the fantasy room. There I find Cristiano standing by the glass wall with a view of the colorful school of fishes swimming by in the aquarium.

He turns to face me with that easy grin and instantly I'm taken back to the thrill of last night.

This is the second time I've seen this man and he's had the same mind-numbing effect on me. Something makes me want to get lost in him. I don't know if it's his dominance, confidence, or presence.

There's just something, and if I'm being honest, there's something about each of them that fascinates me.

I don't know if that's normal, but it's true.

Last night gave me a glimpse of what lies beneath the surface, and I want to see more.

5

MEGAN

As I look at Cristiano, I note how tall, handsome, and muscular he is.

Tonight he's wearing a gray button-down shirt with the sleeves rolled up, revealing the tail of an inky black dragon coiling up his thick forearms. His black pants show off his defined legs and I wonder if he has tattoos there too.

I think he does and he's one of those men who can carry off the tattooed bad boy image, as well as the professional businessman.

Whichever version he shows, I already know it will always display his raw masculine beauty.

"Hello," I say first, pulling myself from my daze. As much as I would love to, I can't stare at him all night. *Or forever.*

Or marvel at how this man has managed to distract me from my problems. Especially after another vile encounter with Bill that's left me feeling like I need to turn my skin inside out and wash it to get clean.

"Hello there, Megan. Come here to me." His deep baritone seeps into every pore of my body and lulls me to him.

When I reach, he leans in and brushes his lips over mine. The kiss pushes a smile to my face and a blush tickles my skin when I taste the hint of alcohol mixed with tobacco.

"Nice and early." His smile revealing perfect white teeth, radiates with confidence. I like it.

I am slightly early, only by five or so minutes. There was no point hanging around the dressing rooms with the girls who were down there getting changed.

I didn't want to talk to anyone, so I just got ready as quickly as I could and left.

"Is early okay?"

"Of course."

"Where are Levi and Knox?"

"They'll be here soon. They're running a little late. They also won't be staying the night, so I have you all to myself. Is that okay?"

"Of course." I borrow his words the same way he borrowed mine, with the knowledge that tonight is going to be very different from last night.

Tonight we'll be having sex, and it was clear from the details Mimi gave me when I arrived that I'm in for another exciting night.

Because they all want to fuck me bareback, she went through a sexual checklist with me in line with the question-naire and sexual health test I'd done before I came back to work here. Basically, she needed to make sure I was still clean and on contraception which I am.

It's part of my contract, which is practically signed in blood, that if I have sex with anyone outside the club, they have to wear a condom.

Realizing I've zoned out, I bring my focus back to Cristiano, remembering I need to thank him for the money before we do or say anything else.

"Thank you for the money," I say, hoping I sound as grateful as I feel.

His eyes hold mine and he's silent for a moment too long. I almost think I've offended him until his lips twitch into a smile.

"Did it help?"

"Yes. It did."

"I guess now we know a little more about each other, Megan Porter." He lingers on each syllable as if he takes pleasure in saying my full name.

"Yes, we do."

Something wicked flashes in his eyes, sending a shiver of fear through me. I've been trying to figure him out since last night. Now that I know what kind of family he's coming from, I'm curious about the sort of man he is.

Is he as dangerous as the other mafia men I've come across?

Are Knox and Levi like him too?

My guess is they are.

"What?" He quirks a hard brow and I school my thoughts.

"Nothing."

My evident nerves bring another smile to his face and he brushes a finger over my cheek, heating my skin.

"You look like you have something to say."

"No." I shake my head. I've already stepped over the line and I need to remember my place.

"You don't have to be scared of me, Megan." He keeps his tone measured and even. "It's clear you've done your research, but if like you say you've been working at this club for a while, then you should be used to my kind. You know that inside the walls of this club, we don't bite unless you want us to. Right?"

"Yes."

"Good girl. Now come take a walk with me." He puts out his hand to take mine and I give it to him. When our fingers entwine, electricity races up my arm.

Anticipation fills every inch of my body as I allow him to lead me through the sliding doors.

This club has all sorts of hidden gems like secret passage-ways and pathways that interconnect. This is one of them. The whole floor is filled with a total of sixty fantasy rooms, some of which are themed. Others, like the one we're approaching, have glass windows so people can watch what's happening inside.

Cristiano leads me over there and we stop by the window to look at the raunchy activities before us.

In the center of the room is a wild orgy of people wearing masquerade masks. I'm guessing there are at least twenty people joined together on the red cushioned mattress in a cacophony of limbs and body parts.

Since the walls aren't completely soundproof like some of the other rooms, their moans filter through to us like an erotic chorus of the forbidden.

To the left and right of the orgy are elegant sofas with more people having sex.

My gaze settles on a woman wearing nothing but a leather bra straddling a man with a Phantom of the Opera mask covering half of his face. Another man wearing a harlequin mask steps up behind her and thrusts deep into her ass.

They both start fucking her and she throws her head back, her body taking their relentless pounds. As she is wearing a mask too, I can't see her face, but from the way her jaw slackens, I can tell she must be experiencing intense pleasure.

It reminds me of the few times I visited the club for fun before I started working here. I didn't know places like this even existed until an adventurous ex of mine gave me the dark intro to the world of those who really live life on the edge.

Despite my debacle, I still like that part. It's the thing that always arouses me.

Cristiano pulls me from my thoughts when he moves behind me and slips an arm around my waist. Leaning closer, he brushes his cheek over my ear and his massive erection pushes against my ass. He's aroused and wants me to know it. I'm aroused too, so when he pushes harder, I move into him, savoring the feeling of his cock pressing against me. I can't help but imagine what he'll feel like inside me.

I glance up at him over my shoulder and notice the fascination dancing in his eyes. There's an electric blue light above us which makes them appear brighter than they already are.

Catching my face, he guides me back to watch the woman and the two men possessing her. She comes, and as I hear her carnal cries of ecstasy, my mouth grows slack with desire.

"You're a voyeur." His voice holds the same fascination I saw lurking in his eyes. His hold loosens and I look at him.

"Am I?" I am, but I'm intrigued how he could know that about me just from the last few minutes.

"Yes, but you're not the kind of woman I'd expect to meet here."

"What kind of woman do you think I am?" Maybe he did look me up.

"You're sexy as fuck, so that part fits." He leans in, wrapping me in the musk of his cologne and his natural masculine scent. "But I can see there's more to you than what you're showing me."

"Did you by any chance do your research on me too?" I'm stepping across another line, but part of me is curious to know if I've interested him too.

His smile widens. "I could have, but I didn't. I like mystery. Sometimes the unknown is enticing." His eyes dim for a moment, clouding his expression, but he resumes control before I can assess what I saw. "Sometimes it's nicer to find things out a bit at a time just from talking."

"I like that too."

"So, what do you like about watching, Miss Voyeur?" He studies my face as if searching for more to learn about me.

I think for a moment and tap into my inner kink. "I like the way people can be when they're free. It's amazing to see what they do when there's no restraint on them and no one to judge them. What about you? What do you like?"

"Everything. And I probably go to places like this more than I should." He chuckles. "I think I'm going to be like this forever."

"What about Knox and Levi?"

"That's yet to be determined, but I think I might be able to vouch for them."

"How long have you guys been friends?" I lean against the rails and stare back at him.

"Since birth. We're all twenty-nine now, so that's a lot of years."

"Wow. That is a long time to be friends." Sadness clogs my throat when I think of Paige, but I regain control of my thoughts so I can focus on the handsome man before me.

"It is."

"And, have you always had the same tastes in women?"

A light chuckle falls from his lips. I'm sure he knows I'm really asking if they've always shared women.

"Yes, we have, but we have rules."

"Like what?"

"Like I always take the lead."

I was right again. "Always?"

"Always. I start and I finish."

"Do you ever do anything with a woman without them?"

"I do. We don't restrict each other from forming relationships. We get that not every woman is going to like being shared. Neither of us has had any relationship that serious though."

It's interesting. I've worked here long enough to see a lot of group sex, but I've never asked questions like this before. "Have you ever liked the same girl?"

"Many times."

"What happens then?"

"We do our best to keep her. That's why I want to book you for the next three weeks."

My jaw drops. "What? Really?"

"Yes. Three weeks at ten grand a night to secure your company and an extra fifty up front to turn down all other offers. What do you think of that?"

Holy. Fucking. Shit.

Three weeks at that kind of money reduces my sentence here to a little under a year and I would be able to pay Bill a quarter million dollars.

Tears of joy sting the backs of my eyes and I have to steady my emotions, so I don't break down.

Cristiano continues to study me. "I hope that sounds like a reasonable offer."

"It definitely is."

"Then say yes to me."

"Yes, absolutely yes." He wouldn't know what this offer means to me.

"Good girl. Because I simply can't wait to feast on you." He presses his lips to mine again for another kiss. This time I melt into him, leaning against his granite chest.

When he runs his hands over my breasts, the wetness between my legs grows, filling my panties. I moan as he squeezes and kneads his fingers into my soft flesh, flicking his thumbs over my nipples.

Then suddenly, he's moving my hand and placing it over his cock. My breath becomes ragged when I feel how hard he is.

"Stroke me." His rusty voice caresses my lips.

Gladly I stroke his cock through his pants and take a moment to watch the pleasure filling his handsome face. Seeing him like this makes me want to please him even more, so I rub his cock harder. A deep grown rumbles in his chest and he claims my lips again with ravenous hunger and greedy desire.

My body yields to the possession. So when he lifts the hem of my negligee and pushes his fingers into my pussy I already know how wet I am.

"You're soaked." He brushes his nose over mine. "Baby, do you need me to fuck you?"

"Yes." I've never wanted anything more, and I don't care how desperate I sound. I do need him.

"Then I think we need to get started."

6

MEGAN

We crash through the doors of the room and Cristiano strips off my clothes.

He keeps his lips on mine as we fall onto the bed and I allow my mind to slip.

My heart races as my body prepares for the newness of being with another man.

A man I'm hungry for.

Hungry?

Christ. I only met Cristiano last night. I shouldn't feel so driven or eager to be with him.

Moving out of the kiss, he pulls his shirt over his head, showing me the rigid muscles and tattoos I imagined were entirely real. His torso is covered in artwork that steals my breath away.

The full body of the dragon I previously spotted coiling up his forearm wraps around his shoulder and spans over the left side of his chest. On his right are a gargoyle and Arabic-looking symbols.

He smiles with satisfaction when he sees me looking. "Like what you see?"

"I love it."

"Here's some more." He shoves his pants and boxers down his legs, revealing his cock and more artistic tattoos splashed over his legs.

The designs are eye-catching, but so is his massive cock bouncing between his legs.

He finishes taking off his clothes and reaches for my ankle to pull me down to the edge of the bed. Then before I can say anything else, he buries his face between my thighs and starts eating out my pussy.

Fuck. It feels amazing. Every stroke of his tongue licking over my clit and pussy lips is enthralling. The thrilling sensation that shoots through me is so powerful I come straightaway, arching off the bed as I lace my fingers through the silky strands of his hair.

As my juices flow, he laps it up, drinking me. The tender yet devouring way he touches me makes me feel like a goddess, and he doesn't stop feasting until he's licked me clean.

"Get on your knees. I haven't seen that ass yet." His eyes sparkle as he speaks.

I smile and roll onto all fours, pushing out my ass. He lands a heavy hand on my ass cheeks, making my hair fall over my face.

"Fucking perfect." He gives me another slap then he gets on the bed, settling behind me.

I quickly glance at him and take in the wild look in his eyes. When he grabs my hips, I turn back to face the wall.

A breath is all I get before he plunges deep inside my

pussy, my body welcoming him as he slams in and buries himself to the hilt.

The air whooshes from my lungs and dangerous heat writhes through me. The kind that could incinerate everything in its path, leaving nothing behind. Cristiano starts moving inside me and fucking hell, I feel like I'm going to come again.

He speeds up, his pumps driving into me savagely as the room fills with the wet erotic sounds of flesh slapping against flesh. My moans and his deep groans join the melody, and wild pleasure takes over, spiraling me to new heights.

My God, I needed this. I needed this. I loathe thinking about Hunter right now, but this moment erases him from my body. After tonight he won't be the last man I was with or the last man I gave myself to. He'll just be a statistic I can forget.

As if Cristiano can sense that my mind has strayed, he fucks me harder. My mind returns to his command, taking his powerful, soul-consuming thrusts.

Every nerve in my body dances with wild, raw heat, and I come again, my cries pouring out of my throat.

"Cristiano!" His name on my lips sounds so natural. Like it was meant to be there. His deep chuckle tells me I've pleased him.

"That's right, scream my name. Say it again."

I do, and I feel like every function of my body is destined to follow his every command.

"Say it again." His voice strains like he's fighting to speak as badly as I am to control the frenzy of thoughts and emotions within me.

"Cris...tiano." My body bows in his arms as shuddering breaths leave my lungs and I come completely undone.

He, on the other hand, is still as solid as iron inside me, but I take what he gives me, craving more and more and more.

He continues his scandalous assault on my body and I grip onto the sheets as arousal coils through me all over again. At that moment, the door opens, and Knox and Levi walk in. Radiant smiles spread across their faces when they see Cristiano pounding into me. I can tell from their fascination they're voyeurs too.

Since I've never had people walk in on me when I'm having my brains fucked out, I expect to feel embarrassed. But I don't.

"Greedy bastard," Knox says with a shake of his head. "Couldn't wait for us."

"I'm not going to blame him. I'd do the same if I were in his shoes." Levi laughs.

My mind is so scrambled from the pleasure Cristiano is giving me as he continues to fuck me that I can't control the moans pouring out of my mouth. When I think of Knox and Levi taking me just like this, streaks of red-hot pleasure liquify my brain.

"You'd better jump in before I decide to keep her for myself," Cristiano replies in that same strained voice.

"Greedy motherfucker, we're not going to let you do that," Knox counters instantly.

Cristiano continues to pound into me while Knox and Levi take off their clothes. When their shirts come off, I notice their bodies are tattooed as well, with similar designs as Cristiano.

When they take off their pants and their cocks jut free, all thoughts of tattoos evaporate from my mind. The two are as hung as Cristiano.

Cristiano pulls out of me when Knox and Levi join us, but he doesn't release his grip on my hips.

"You still with me, Goddess?" The scruff of his jaw tickles my cheek when he whispers in my ear.

"I'm with you," I manage, loving being called *goddess*.

"Good girl. It's their turn now, but I get to be the only one to finish inside your pussy tonight. Understand?"

"Yes."

"Now, please us."

He helps me stand, and as they gather around me with raw desire darkening their eyes, I know what they want. They want me. The knowledge sends a tremor of excitement through me.

Knox pulls me in for a kiss with those big strong arms and his dick brushes against my thigh. I reach for it and stroke him as he kisses me. The same fire that scorched my brain when I was with Cristiano burns me and I find it mesmerizing. They're two different guys. How can it feel the same?

Before I fall into a mindless stupor of delight, he chuckles and passes me to Levi who also kisses me.

Last night must have been a taste of what this man wanted to give me because as his tongue captures mine, it feels wild and rebellious.

It's only when warm hands grab my waist from behind that I'm taken back to reality. I pull away from Levi when I realize it's Cristiano holding me.

"Levi, stop hogging the girl. You two can have all the time you want to play later."

"It's not my fault if she likes me more." Levi chuckles.

"Like fuck she does," Knox interrupts, reaching out to squeeze my breasts while Cristiano cups my sex.

"What if I liked all of you just the same?" I giggle.

"That works extremely well." Cristiano licks my cheek.

"How about you show us just how much you like us, Goddess." Knox winks and when Cristiano releases me, I drop to my knees, knowing exactly what to do next to please them.

The guys look at each other as if I just scored major points.

Knox runs a hand over my head, lacing his fingers through my hair, so I take his cock first. I lick the tip where pre-cum has already started to form, swirling my tongue around the bulbous head before I take him into my mouth and start sucking him.

He continues to stroke my head and the rapturous look of pleasure on his handsome face encourages me to keep sucking, so I do.

When it looks like he's getting the right amount of pleasure, I start stroking Levi's cock while I continue sucking Knox.

Cristiano crouches behind me and massages my breasts with one hand, tweaking my nipples. He rubs my clit with his other hand, gliding from my pussy to the tight rosette of my asshole.

His hands on me feel so fucking amazing, but so are the thrusts of Knox's cock in my mouth and the hardness of Levi's cock in my hands. I didn't think I could feel any better than I already did.

The sight of us together must be so hot and forbidden and so completely the dark fantasy this club was made for.

Cristiano starts sucking my breasts and I move my pussy over his hand, rubbing my clit as pleasure rises within me.

Before I switch to sucking Levi's cock, I give Cristiano a quick kiss on his lips, and then I return my focus to Levi.

I suck his cock and give Knox a hand job at the same time. I keep going, doing what I think will please them and it seems to work.

Cristiano, in the meantime, continues giving me pleasure switching between sucking my breasts and finger fucking me.

We stay like that for a few moments, caught in the pleasure of tasting and touching each other, until Cristiano stands.

I realize he guides the activities the same way he leads with everything else, and standing means it's his turn.

I follow the lead and shuffle to give him my attention.

As I take his cock into my mouth, I taste myself on his length from us fucking around before the guys arrived.

I suck him, giving him the attention I think he needs while the guys start fisting their dicks.

Gliding my tongue over his length, I lick right over the skin of his shaft and then around to his balls.

"You are too perfect," he grates out.

"More than perfect," Levi concedes, crouching down. "It's time I taste these delicious tits." He fills his palms with my left breast and sucks. Knox takes the other one and the two suck on my tits as if they want to devour me.

Cristiano catches my jaw, beckoning me to stop, so I do, and Knox and Levi pause their sucking too.

"It's time to fuck you again," Cristiano says. He glances at Knox and I take that to mean it's his turn.

The look Knox gives me when I gaze at him sends a shockwave of arousal writhing through my body.

He takes my hand and helps me stand. Then instead of putting me back on the bed, he ushers me over to the sofa.

Knox guides me to lie on my side while he sits beside me and sets himself on his side too. He pulls me closer, then slides his cock into me. He starts moving inside me slowly as if caressing my walls as they stretch to take his length. When he starts fucking me, Levi joins us, lifting the upper part of my body onto his lap so I can suck his cock.

While I suck him, Cristiano comes up to me and I stroke his cock.

My blood, simmering with desire, races through my veins as if someone added a dose of napalm to it.

The four of us together like this feels like the perfect synchronicity. Usually, it takes me a while to warm up to someone, even when there's chemistry right off the bat. But this feels like I'm getting everything I've ever wanted from a man, except in three separate parts. I haven't known them for any time at all, but each of them gives me something I need. The emotions flowing through me are so potent I know this isn't just about the work or the money. Everything is real.

Knox pounds into me harder and I come. As I do, I feel his cock go harder inside me and my walls tighten around his length. A low guttural growl rips from his throat as he seems to fight off his own release.

"Fuck, I need to switch out," Knox groans, pulling out of me.

"I can help with that," Levi answers.

I'm barely able to catch my breath when he picks me up and settles me onto his cock so I can straddle him.

Riding Levi's cock while I stare into his gorgeous brown eyes is a treat and I take the opportunity to kiss him. We kiss until my hair is gently tugged. I know without looking it's Cristiano again.

I glance at him and he claims my lips.

Knox moves closer, so I stroke his cock while he lowers to kiss my neck.

Everything between us is so insane and wild I can't get enough.

When Cristiano runs his fingers over my asshole and pushes inside, I know what he means to do to me. He wants to take me with Levi at the same time and fuck my ass.

I expect him to do that, but he doesn't. I'm surprised when he allows Knox to take the lead instead.

Knox takes hold of my hips and massages my asshole while Cristiano gets a tube of lube.

He smears it on me and Levi slows his pumps so Knox can push his cock into my ass.

It hurts like hell, like fire and pleasure rolled into one, like I'm being destroyed but consumed at the same time. I'm being stretched in the best possible ways, and the combination of pleasure and pain is so intense I cry out.

"It's okay, baby. We'll make you feel good soon," Levi promises.

I can't answer. My voice is gone to the same place my mine ran to.

Cristiano sucks my breast, creating a distraction from the pain. I can feel the wetness growing in my passage again and the instant it gushes out of my pussy, Knox slides deeper into my asshole.

The pain subsides and I feel amazing again, the raw dose of pleasure consuming me.

Cristiano kisses my neck and I hold his hand while Knox

and Levi fuck me. Then it's like hands are everywhere, touching me, grabbing me, holding me.

I've lost track of how many times I've come already tonight. I'm coming again and this time, it feels like something drains from my body.

"Switch out, boys, I'm fucking coming," Levi groans.

Knox lifts me while keeping his cock deep in my ass and Cristiano takes Levi's place.

We're right back to where we started, him and I, and this position feels more intimate than when he took me from behind.

Knox continues pounding into my ass while Cristiano is in my pussy. Holding me, he leans back against the sofa, taking me with him so Levi can hoist himself onto it and push his cock into my mouth.

Levi fists my hair and fucks my mouth so hard tears stream down my cheeks, then his cock jerks, and he comes with a savage growl sounding like a wild animal.

His hot cum hits the back of my throat and I swallow it. At the same time, Knox comes in my ass. Cristiano pounds up into me, staying for as long as he can hold out and when he comes, he tightens his grip on me and we both come together.

I collapse onto Cristiano's chest, feeling spent like someone dosed me with pure exhaustion. Never in my entire time working here have I experienced anything like these three men. We did everything tonight, everything.

A warm hand flutters over my back. It's Cristiano.

"Are you still with us, Goddess?" he asks.

As tired as I am, I would never say no. "I'm with you."

"Good, because we're just getting started and we want to devour you."

7

CRISTIANO

Megan presses her dainty hands against the granite wall of the shower.

As she arches her back, allowing the water to run down her smooth skin, I slam my dick into her tight little pussy. Then I pound into her like this is the first time we're fucking.

Even after the guys and I exhausted her, she's still taking what I give her.

We've been together for hours. The guys left just before midnight and it's now three in the morning.

I can't remember the last time I stayed at the club all night. I'd planned to have one session of fun and then head home, but when Megan arrived, my mind changed swiftly.

Tonight was amazing. *Megan* was fucking amazing. I know Knox and Levi felt it too. Now I have her all to myself and I don't want the sun to come up. I don't want to step away from this fantasy and go back to the shit I'm dealing with when it comes to my grandfather.

If not for the incredibly late meeting the guys had with

one of our VIP clients, I know they would have wanted to stay the night too to indulge in the beauty.

They'll be happy when I tell them I'll be booking her for three weeks. Even if the gesture is more for me than for them. They both like her, so they'll see her as a treat.

I figured she'll be able to provide some much-needed therapy after I hit them with the news of my grandfather's marriage demands.

I plan to tell them later when we meet. I'm not looking forward to it.

Pushing the thought out of my mind, I focus on the beautiful woman in my arms. As I hammer into her luscious body, I allow myself to get lost in her and I can tell she does the same with me.

I know when a woman is fucking me because she wants something like money, power, or just being seen with me. None of that is here.

Megan is actually giving herself to me, and the only thing I can see her taking from me is the same thing I'm taking from her—*the distraction.*

Her need for it is, however, unlike mine because I can sense she's in trouble.

Many of the girls who work here are, and the club is like a fucking conduit to sign your soul away. It's where you come when you have no option but to sell your body.

Within moments of meeting Megan, I knew she needed serious money. If she didn't, she wouldn't have accepted my offer to be shared by a dangerous group of men like us.

Distracting myself with her has worked, but it's doing other things to me too I didn't ask for. Like wanting to know more about her. And caring. I saw the way she looked when I made the offer. She almost cried.

The gratitude in her eyes made me want to cross the line and pry deeper into why she's here.

She climaxes, throwing her head back and arching against me. The walls of her pussy wrap around my dick like a vice and as my balls draw up, I come too.

The goddess milks me clean, sending thrills racing over my body.

Fuck... this has to be the last time.

I need to stop and remember what this is and what it's not. Every time I try to though, she touches me, and like some siren, she lulls me back into her.

When her knees buckle, I slip an arm around her waist to steady her.

She's reached her limit. Maybe she reached it hours ago and me being the selfish bastard kept her going.

As I pull her to me and she smiles over her shoulder, I notice how exhausted she looks. But beneath her exhaustion is more desire.

"You're fucking perfect." I speak into her hair, inhaling the scent of strawberries and honey. I don't know how often I've told her how perfect she is tonight, but each time she's blushed as if it's the first she's hearing it.

"Thank you. You are too."

"Thanks, baby." I'm not perfect. Nothing is further from the truth, but I'll take the compliment because it's from her. "You need to sleep now."

"I'm fine. I'm not tired." Her voice sounds weary. A complete contrast to what she's telling me.

"You can barely keep your eyes open."

"I like this."

Me too, but I mustn't, and neither must she. "Bad girl."

"I'm sorry."

"No, you aren't." I turn her to face me and kiss her.

Since one of us needs to take control, I decide it should be me. So I pick her up and carry her back into the room.

I grab some towels and take the opportunity to dry her off before I do myself, then we fall into the bed.

This is the part where I should leave. It's at the very least an opening for me to exit the fantasy and whatever spell she has on me, but when we start kissing again, it's clear I have no intention of leaving this bed.

She kisses me like she can't get enough and wants all of me. It becomes so intense I have to pull back and stare at her. Megan notices I've regained control and schools the desire on her face.

I stare at her for a few moments, trapping myself in her gaze. The soft amber light from the dim room is bright enough for me to see the emotion beyond her beauty. It makes me want to peel away the layers and delve in.

When her bright brown eyes sparkle with need, I run a finger across the deep

valley between her breasts. "You want me again."

"Is that such a bad thing?" She giggles, stifling a yawn.

"No."

"I'm just…"

"What?"

"Having a good time. I had a good time with you and the guys. I mean it."

Her lids grow heavy.

"We did too. Now I want you to sleep."

"Will you lie next to me?"

"Yes."

I rest my head next to hers and within seconds of closing her eyes, she falls asleep. I sleep too, enjoying what I can.

When I wake up, I have to put some kind of plan in action.

I just don't know where the fuck to start.

I walk into my office and set my cappuccino down on my desk.

The guys should be here in a minute. I'm sure they'll be buzzing about Megan the same way I am.

It will be a shame to talk about anything that's not her, but we need to talk about what's happening.

I thought it was a given that my grandfather would hand over the business to me, so I made Knox and Levi several promises. They worked their asses off to make sure we succeeded. That's why I have to figure this out.

I know our friendship doesn't mean they'll always have to follow me. Each of them has the capacity and ability to be leaders of their own empires. If I fail and they left Rivera Developments, I couldn't fault them. I would have to go too because I wouldn't be able to work under Lorenzo.

The door swings open and they come in wearing the same smiles from last night.

"Asshole, where's our coffee?" Knox chuckles

I shake my head at him. "Sorry, man, it slipped my mind."

"Or maybe your head was otherwise occupied." Levi throws me a mischievous look. "What time did you leave the club?"

"Not long ago."

The two exchange their habitual glances of curiosity, then look back at me.

"You like her." Knox points a finger at me and nods.

"So do you guys."

"We do. I just can't remember the last time you spent the entire night at the club, so I'm wondering if we've come to that point of decision."

The point of decision is what we agreed to in high school when we started sharing women. The agreement is that we'd each understand if any of us met a woman we didn't want to share or no longer wanted to share.

The three of us have had several women over the years and none of us have reached that point yet. I haven't now.

"No." I shake my head.

"Good. We all had fun with her last night." Levi sits in the chair in front of me and amplifies his smile. "Please tell me you booked her again tonight."

"I've booked her for the next three weeks." I decided on three weeks because we'll be in charge while my grandfather is in New Orleans. After that, we'll all be busy again traveling. We won't be going to Europe. We'll each have shorter trips, but we'll still be busy.

"Fuck yeah." Levi bumps his fist with Knox.

I want to smile too, but I don't. It's time for business.

"Guys, we have to talk." The moment I say that, the air shifts and the smiles fade from their faces.

"What's going on? That sounds serious. Don't tell me we pissed off the old man." Knox looks me over with keen eyes. He's the observant one, so I'm not surprised by his remark.

I run a heavy hand threw my hair and sit on the edge of my desk.

"We haven't pissed him off yet." I take a quick sip of air and fill them in on my grandfather's request.

"What the hell are you going to do?" Levi's voice holds the same edge of worry I feel.

"Other than finding an Evelina to marry him, what is he supposed to do?" Knox points out the obvious.

"But that three-year shit is going to be the kick."

"Don't I know it." I crack my knuckles. "My grandfather isn't stupid and he knows what I'm like. He thought this through well enough to lock me down on all sides. He wants me to have a real relationship, not something I can buy with money."

Knox looks at me. "What are you thinking, Cristiano? Don't fucking tell me you're going to allow Lorenzo to take the company or fucking marry your cousin. Simona will hate you and forgive me for saying she'd be right."

"I'm not going to let either of those things happen. My grandfather is out of line for this, so I plan to fight fire with fire." Even if I don't want to disrespect him. "I need to find a woman who is suitable enough to help me pull this off. Someone I can trust to stay in the game for three years."

"Then I suggest we start making a list of potential candidates." Levi rests his hands on his knees.

"I'll do the list," Knox cuts in. "Maybe you can assess the potentials and we can take it from there."

Levi bobs his head. "I can do that."

"Whatever we do has to be fast." I blow out a ragged breath. "My grandfather wants to meet Evelina when he comes back from New Orleans."

So we have three weeks to find her.

8

KNOX

Megan has been talking to me about the music she likes while Cristiano and Levi went to get more drinks.

Tonight we've taken our party of four out to the club floor in one of the VIP lounges. The guys and I are wearing masks and Megan looks like our porcelain doll.

From where we're sitting, we can see the people below on the dance floor partying away and those on the sidelines having wild sex.

Megan's knees brush against mine as her chatter about the Kings of Leon becomes more animated. I like that band too, but I'm more of a heavy metal kind of guy. For her, though, I'll listen to her talk about anything.

It's been a while since any woman has had this effect on me. I know Cristiano and Levi feel the same way. Having Megan around has helped take the stress off this marriage shit.

It's been nearly two weeks since we've been working on finding a suitable *Evelina*. The whole thing has stressed me out because I'm not sure if we can find the right woman. I think it's going to take a lot of work to outsmart an old fox like Cristiano's grandfather, who's been in the game longer than we have. We've all been on edge because the time is drawing closer for his return.

Megan smiles and looks at me as if she's waiting for me to answer a question. A question I haven't heard.

"You didn't hear me did you?" She giggles, tucking a lock of her shiny black hair behind her ear.

"Sorry, babe, I'm a little distracted tonight." I shouldn't be. Not with her. She's beautiful and with her lips painted red like that, she looks like a work of art.

"Are you okay?"

I've wanted to ask her the same thing since I met her, but I held back. "I'm fine."

We've all sensed she needed the money and hoped that what she gets from us would be enough to fix whatever situation she's in. We still haven't checked her out. We promised we wouldn't even though we've wanted to.

There are enough rules about boundaries and privacy to keep the fantasy alive, but there comes a time when human emotion takes over and opens the door to curiosity.

"So, I'm guessing if you zoned out, Kings of Leon might not be your thing."

I lean forward and lift a lock of her hair. "Not so much, but I like that you like it."

She laughs and it's a pretty, innocent sound. When you come from a world as dark as mine, you notice differences like that.

"Well, I guess that's good." She rests her hands on her lap.

"What else do you like, Goddess?"

She thinks for a moment. "I like...helping people."

"In what ways, baby?"

"Talking through their problems."

"You sound like a shrink." It was meant to be a joke, but the coy look on her face suggests that idea might not be so farfetched for her.

"Shrinks aren't that bad."

"No, I suppose not. Is that what you want to do?"

She nods and there's a sadness in her eyes I haven't seen before. The guard she places up when she's with us drops and I can see the pain in her soul.

"I was a year away from qualifying as a therapist."

I digest this new piece of information about her, taking note of the way she spoke in the past tense. Of course, now I want to know why she's not pursuing her career.

"What happened, baby?"

"I had some things happen that set me back."

I don't have to ask if that's why she's here. I sense it from the nerves that have just filled her expression. "Will you get to finish your studies soon?"

"I hope so. It's my dream. I've been working toward it for a long time."

I lift my half-finished glass of drink and raise a toast to her. "Then here's to your dreams coming true."

"Thank you. That means a lot." A sweet smile lifts the corners of her doll-like mouth and she leans forward to kiss me. The kiss is too chaste for where we are and far too innocent for a man like me.

At that moment, Levi and Cristiano come back with our drinks and set them on the table.

When Levi takes Megan's hand and leads her away to the dance floor, I think about how she looked when she spoke about her dream.

I knew there was more to her when we first met. So

hearing she's a scholar is no surprise. Being a therapist or something of that caliber suits her.

So what sent her to this club to sell her body to men like us?

As I gaze out at her on the dancefloor dancing with Levi, I note how carefree she looks amongst the other bodies clashing together. It's her who looks like she's escaping life. But with us.

From her personality, it's clear she's a good girl, and even though she has a wild side, she shouldn't be in a place like this.

I look back at Cristiano and when I think of his marriage debacle, a very bad idea forms in my head.

What if Megan became Evelina?

We thought it would be best to pick a woman that Cristiano has known for a while and trusted. But maybe that wasn't such a good idea because most of the women he knows can't be trusted. That's the reason we can't find anyone suitable.

Maybe we've been looking in all the wrong places when what we're looking for could be right here.

I think Megan would be perfect.

Cristiano stares back at me from across the table.

We're in a booth at the back of the coffeehouse opposite the Dark Odyssey.

It's eight in the morning and I've just laid my idea about Megan on the table.

At least Levi is looking at me with a spark of interest, which tells me he's on board. Cristiano, on the other hand, not so much.

"You seriously think I should ask *Megan*?" He steeples his hands and glares at me, pressing his lips into a thin line.

"Yes."

"What about the women on the list?"

"They're still there. I just think we should consider her."

"I kind of think she's perfect too," Levi adds.

"How?" Cristiano cuts him a stern glance. "She supposed to be temporary."

"Fuck off. You and I both know you don't want her to be fucking temporary."

He doesn't argue about that. Instead, he sets his hands on the table. "I don't think it's a good idea. Why do you?"

"Because she's not from our world and we seem to have this bond going on with her."

I nod, agreeing. "Exactly. And we already know she needs money."

"I don't want to take advantage of that." The tentative expression on his face suggests he cares about her. During the time I've known him, there have only been a handful of women Cristiano has claimed to care about.

"Cristiano, if she's desperate, she'll most likely be grateful for the offer." I know whoever he picks will be compensated heavily, so it might as well be a woman we care about.

It was me who made the booking that first night we met Megan. When I spoke to Mimi, she recommended her. As the nights have gone by, I've realized why. I also realized that she didn't just recommend her. She picked us because Mimi

knew we'd like Megan and want to book her. She also knew we were likely to make Megan a good offer. That means she would get whatever money she needed faster.

"She likes all of us and we like her. That has to count for

something." I think it's valid to point that out. "At least think about it."

He gazes at the groves on the table, a war of thoughts battling through his mind.

"Alright." Cristiano straightens and his eyes meet mine. "I'll think about it."

9

MEGAN

It's my last night with the guys.

I've tried not to think about how final tonight will be and how sad I'll feel when I don't see them anymore.

I know it's crazy, but I really do like all three of them. Being with them has been like living in my own fantasy. Over the last three weeks, they've healed my broken heart.

As I make my way down the corridor, excitement bubbles in me just at the thought of seeing them.

We're using the same room we used the first night we met.

This morning I woke to the final balance of two hundred and ten thousand in my account.

I went to pay Bill before coming here, and just like the other week, he had his snide comments. I didn't care. Paying all that money gave me a boost.

I still have a hell of a lot left to pay, but at least I don't owe half a million dollars anymore.

My heels click against the marble floors as I approach the room and I catch sight of my reflection in the glass walls.

The flowing white dress hugging my body with its plunging neckline makes me look like I'm going on some fancy date on a yacht. This was what the guys wanted me to wear, so it's anyone's guess what they've planned tonight.

I look good, better than I have in months. My face isn't as gaunt, and the dark circles under my eyes have faded.

I open the door and find Cristiano standing by the little bar area with a bottle of wine. Two glasses are already laid out. He's shaved and trimmed his hair, but it still has a wild look that's sexy. Like most nights, he's dressed in full black.

The fantasy begins the moment our eyes lock. I skip into his arms and he kisses me.

"You look beautiful." He strokes my lips with his.

"Thank you." I grin, then look around for Knox and Levi. "Where are the others?"

"It's just going to be us tonight." Something that looks like nervousness flashes across his face. It throws me because the emotion seems out of place on him.

"Oh. So I won't see them again?"

"We'll arrange something. I have something to ask you and I just needed it to be you and me tonight to talk."

"Talk?" I lift my brows. I can't imagine talking or a night passing when we don't have sex.

"Yes, talk."

"You've paid a pretty hefty price just to talk to me."

"Tonight will be slightly different because of what I have to discuss. Come and sit." He motions to the sofa area, then places a hand on the small of my back to usher me over.

We sit so we're facing each other and I stare openly at him. "I'm all ears." *And nerves.* This feels quite mysterious.

"First, I want to ask you a few questions."

"Like what?"

"Like how much money you might need before you stop working here."

"Oh, I see. Those questions."

"I don't mean to pry into your business, but I just want to know."

My eyes cling to his as I mull over how to answer him. I can't tell him the truth, so I think of the only thing I can say.

"I need a lot of money. I...found myself in a situation where this was the only way out."

His brows crease. "Are you in trouble, Megan?"

I almost laugh. I might if he wasn't so right. "I'm handling it."

"Megan, if you're in trouble, you should tell me." The blue of his eyes darken with a wealth of concern that touches my heart and I wish I could tell him what's happened to me. I almost wonder if it would be okay, but I hold back like I have been because I don't know if I'd be doing more harm to myself than good.

I do have a handle on the situation because I've been paying Bill, so maybe it's best to err on the side of caution.

"Things were bad, but I'm okay now. You've helped me more than you know. I'm hoping by next year I'll be back on track to where I need to be."

"One year?" His brows lift. "What happens after?"

"I get to start over or hopefully pick up where I left off." My shoulders relax at the welcoming thought of freedom.

"Well...I have another offer for you. Something that might help you start over sooner or pick up where you left off."

"Another offer?" He already had my attention, but now I'm hanging on to every syllable of his words.

"Yes, but because it's something that will bind you to me for more than a year, I want you to think about it."

That sounds mysterious. "What's the offer?"

He releases a steady breath. "It's five million dollars to marry me and stay married to me for three years."

My blood freezes in my veins. There's no way I heard him say what I think I heard.

"What? What did you say?"

"I need you to marry me, Megan, and stay married to me for three years. If you agree, I'll pay the first million up front and the rest at the end of the three years."

"Oh my God. You're serious?"

"I'm very serious." He opens his palms, then knits his fingers together. "I'm supposed to take over my family business, but my grandfather wants me to get married before I do."

My head is spinning. As I think of the crazy amount of money five million dollars is and all I could do with it, every atom in my body comes alive.

I'd be debt free and I could do everything I ever wanted. I could find my stepfather and continue investigating my mother's death.

But... doing this—marrying him—would be a big deal.

It's easy to close your eyes and shun the little things that usually mean something to you when you're desperate.

Like the fact that marriage for me meant being with someone you love forever.

I was married to Hunter only a few months ago. When we said I do, I saw happiness. I saw love. I saw hope and dreams we would accomplish together.

Although marriage has left a dark mark on my soul, I still see all those things.

"I can see you're processing this. I know it's a lot." He reaches out and runs a thumb over my knuckle. "Don't give me an answer now. Go home and think. I just need an answer by Saturday."

Two days. "Okay, I'll do that." I'd be crazy to turn him down, but I suppose it's wise to take the time to think if I'm being offered it.

"Don't come back to the club until you give me an answer. I'll compensate you."

He stands, plants a kiss on my forehead, then leaves.

I stare at the wall and think of what five million could do for me.

I like Cristiano a lot. And I don't think being married to him would mean not being with Levi and Knox. Although he didn't mention them, I can't see him stopping the good thing we have going on when we're all together for the sake of marriage. I'm sure he thought of me as a good candidate because of that.

There's also the glaringly obvious fact that I like them all.

I do, but... am I seriously thinking about this?

How would it look to get married again so soon after Hunter? But fuck, who cares? I don't have anybody to care about me now. Look at me. I'm working in a sex club because I had no hope and no one to turn to.

It's five million dollars, Megan...

Pushing to my feet, I decide to head out. I don't want to be here if I don't have to be. And that kind of sums everything else up.

Why would I be here if I don't need to be? If Cristiano can get me out of here, I should grab that offer by the reigns and ride the fuck out of hell.

I just don't know if it would be as simple as that. After all, he's Cristiano Rivera. I'd be married to a mafia boss for three years.

It could be jumping out of the frying pan and landing in the infernal flames of hell.

I change my clothes and head to my car, getting lost in my thoughts again when the cool night air floats over my skin.

I'm so deep in concentration I don't realize someone is walking far too close behind me until it's too late.

When a large hand clamps around my wrist, I whirl around, coming face to face with Chad, one of Bill's crew of deranged henchmen. Abel and Dillon, the other part of the trio step out of the shadows and my body goes numb as they surround me.

What the hell are they doing here?

"What do you want?" I cry, trying to wrench my arm free. This shouldn't be happening. I paid all that money earlier today. There shouldn't be any problems at all. However, the ferocious look on Chad's face tells me otherwise.

"The boss isn't pleased you're here fucking other men." Chad's gravelly voice tightens the knots in my stomach. "He thinks you can pay the rest of that debt by fucking him instead. So we've come to take you."

"No, let me go!" I yank my arm away, but he tightens his grip on my wrist and secures an arm around my waist.

Frantically I glance back to the door I came from, hoping someone will see what's happening to me. But nobody comes out, and nobody probably will. This is the staff parking area and most of the people working will be in the club until the early hours of the morning.

A van pulls up with another one of Bill's henchmen at the wheel. The moment I see him, I know I'm screwed.

"Let go of me!" I scream, but Chad covers my mouth and drags me toward the van.

When he lifts me off the ground, I realize I can't escape. I have no energy, no hope, no chance. Tears of desolation pour out of my eyes as the van door flies open. Just then, the sound of a gunshot rips through the night and something wet splashes on me.

Chad's hand falls from my mouth and his hold on me loosens.

I fall to the ground at the same time he does and I see he's been shot in the head and that wetness I felt was blood. It's on me.

More shots fire and Dillon and Abel jump into action. I scramble away to safety, the gravel on the path scraping my knees.

I get behind a blue Ferrari and that's when I see Cristiano running down the path with his gun raised.

He kills Dillon and Abel when they rush forward and the guy in the van doesn't even get a chance to drive away. A bullet lodged in the back of his head just as he gunned the engine.

Cristiano rushes to my side, gathering me up in his arms. Tears of relief flow from my soul as he holds me, but the weight of what nearly happened fractures my mind and breaks me.

At that moment, I realize I was never going to be free.

10

LEVI

My blood is still simmering when I get to Cristiano's house. I wanted to come from last night when he told me what happened to Megan. But when he tasked Knox and me with finding out why in the ever-loving fuck Bill's men tried to kidnap her, I knew I had a higher calling.

When we dug around and found out what's been happening to Megan and how she knows Bill, I wished like hell I'd checked her out sooner. Especially when we all sensed she must have been working at the club because she was in trouble.

There's not a damn thing I can't find out on a person, so I would have been able to confirm she was in deep shit. Deeper than I know she even realized.

Knox left me a few hours ago to come here while I did a bit more digging around.

I make my way to the living room and find Megan sitting in the armchair. Knox is on her left, stroking her neck while Cristiano hands her a cup of coffee.

Her eyes are red and swollen like little slits on her face. She tries to smile when she sees me, but it looks like it hurts.

"Baby," I mutter, moving over to her. I crouch down and plant a kiss on her forehead. "Are you okay?"

"I'm okay." Her voice is barely audible and shaky.

Cristiano looks at me and I nod, silently confirming I've done all I can for the moment.

He knows Megan was married to Hunter Reid, a motherfucker who we're sure was killed by someone in the mob. He also knows the money he gave her went to Bill and everything else I found out is not good by any means.

Hunter was a sort of middle man—and spy—for a number of organizations, from the Bratva to the Cartel. Some of which were enemies to each other. So no fucking wonder his ass is dead. When things go wrong, men like Hunter are always the first to have a target on their backs.

We found out a lot, but we'd still like her to talk to us just to be sure we haven't missed anything.

"I'm going to make breakfast in a few minutes," Cristiano says to her. "Do you need anything else before I start?"

"No. Um... I know you're waiting for me to talk and I should. It's just difficult." She looks at each of us, but her gaze settles on me. "I guess by now you probably know some stuff about me."

The comment doesn't surprise me. She knows I'm the tech of the group and probably guessed I'm only arriving now because I was checking things out.

"We do," I confirm, tilting my head to the side. "It would be helpful to hear what you've been going through, but only if you can talk about it."

"I want to. I just don't know where to start."

"How about with Hunter?" Cristiano suggests and she

74

looks at him. It's clear from the weary way she sets the coffee cup down on the table that her dead husband is her least favorite subject. "How did you meet him?"

"High school. I lost touch with him then we reconnected earlier last year. I was so happy to have him back in my life that I never questioned anything. He just wanted to hurt me."

She takes a quick breath then tells us everything about Hunter, her marriage, the shit he left behind with Bill, and how she ended up at the club. We listen to her pour out her heart, watch her open up, and trust us. By the time she's done talking, I want to erase the pain I can see in her and fix her broken heart.

Most people know me as a killer and would be shocked to hear me voice those types of thoughts. I'm shocked at myself because I've never met a woman who could instill those types of feelings in me. A quick look at Knox and Cristiano and I know they feel the same. When you've been friends as long as we have, you know things without them being said.

So I know we each think of her as ours. Ours to protect, no matter how long we've known her.

"I've had a rough life and this just feels like another kick to push me down." Megan dabs away the tears streaming down her cheeks with the heel of her hand.

I pass her some tissues and give her hand a gentle squeeze. I'm aware of the difficult life she's referring to. In my checks, I found out about her mother's death and her quest to find her stepfather. I haven't told Knox or Cristiano about that part yet, but I will because I think I might be able to help her.

I know Gibbs, the PI she worked with. I contacted him earlier this morning and got the files he had on her stepfather. The fact that Gibbs has searched for him and failed to find him says a lot. Gibbs is industry best and widely used by a number of crime families in the Chicago alliance. However, I like to think of myself as a little bit more above board than Gibbs because I won't think twice about killing a man to get what I need.

.

"Let's eat breakfast now," Cristiano says. "Then Knox will go with you to sort out this thing with Bill."

"Sort out?" Megan's brows shoot up as she tries to process what he means.

"Yes. We'll talk some more when you get back. Okay?"

"Okay... thank you. Thank you all."

Cristiano looks over at me. "While they're out, fill me in on everything else."

"Of course."

There's a lot to tell him and more to sort out because it wasn't Bill who killed Hunter. He just took advantage of the situation to cash in on Megan.

We have worse people to worry about.

11

CRISTIANO

"What else did you find out?" I keep my gaze fixed on Levi. We're sitting on the terrace and I have the crisp morning air surrounding me, but I'm burning up with rage. I feel like an idiot for not doing my checks on Megan.

I don't want to think about what could have happened last night if I hadn't saved her. I was only on that side of the building because I'd run into Salvatore Giordano, Mimi's husband. We had a brief exchange where we arranged to meet up and it was when he left that I heard Megan scream.

"It's not good, Cristiano." Levi bites the inside of his lip. "First of all, Bill was working with Sergei Baranov from the Korolev Bratva."

"Fuck." There are only certain Bratva brotherhoods we work with and the Korolev is not one of them. Mainly because they're into the flesh trade and are a bunch of savages, who will kill their own mothers just to prove a point.

"Bill had no intention of releasing her from her debt. He had big plans for her."

"Like what?" I ball my hand into a tight fist.

"He and Sergei planned to sell her. Sell her for sex until she's all used up, then kill her and sell her organs."

My chest tightens like a large hand is clamped around my lungs squeezing the air out of them.

"Last night happened because she paid all that money," he adds. "He wanted her for himself, but he also knew that she could only get money like what she was paying from someone powerful."

Fucking hell. "I'm going to have to make a few calls." Because Sergei won't speak to anyone in La Cosa Nostra, I'll have to liaise with some of the Pakhans—Bratva leaders—I know in the alliance. Mikhail Dmitriyev is the Pakhan of the New York Brotherhood, so he'd be the best option, but I'm closer to Aiden Romanov, who leads the Voirik in L.A. Lucca Dyshekov is also in L.A. and another good option because of the work he's done across the Bratva as a whole.

I'll speak to all three of them and see who can help me the quickest. One or all of them will be close enough to Sergei to reason with him so I can get Megan off his radar.

"What about Hunter? Do you know who killed him?"

"No, but I have a few ideas. The week before his death, I found emails between him and a dealer from the Perez Cartel. He seemed to be arranging a drug drop, but he was going to steal a box of heroin from Xio Wong of the Yakuzza."

What a fucking idiot Hunter was. Chances are, someone found out about that drug drop. Did he seriously think he could steal from people like that? "So it could be the Yakuzza?"

"It would make sense on the mystery around his death. If it were anyone in the Sicilian mafia, I would have known by now. Probably the same with the Bratva. But, I also saw messages mentioning people like Emilio Vittorio, Judas Kane, and Barabbas Ponteix. It seems Hunter stole from them too or fucked with their clients."

My eyes go wide. Aside from Emilio, who is one of the leaders of the Camorra, the others work with terrorist organizations and motherfuckers who deal with anything black market-related. Essentially, people no one wants to fuck with. This could officially be above me, but I won't allow it.

"This is fucking bull shit."

"Yes, and you know how this works when serious money is owed to certain people."

Yes, I know all too well how things work. There are those like Bill and Sergei who will strike at the first opportunity to recoup their debt. Even if the debt is a fucking dollar, they'll take everything. Then there are others who feel like they've been wronged so severely that they'll lie in wait until you have something they think will fully compensate them. They're the ones to worry about because they do shit like kill your firstborn or massacre an entire family, or kidnap and torture you and the most vulnerable people you know.

"I'll speak to Emilio," I say, formulating a plan. Emilio Vittorio hates my guts, but he did business with my father many years ago. Hopefully, that will count for something. He also loves selling on the black market, so maybe I could kill two birds with one stone if he knows how to reach Judas and Barabbas. "You find a contact for the Perez Cartel and the Yakuzza. Tell them Megan Porter is under my care and the protection of the alliance. She is not to be harmed in any way."

Levi nods. Anyone who goes against that will officially start a war. I don't know anyone who wants that because the threat of a war will fuck with businesses and allies alike, not just in the US but internationally.

"There's one last thing."

My interest piques. "What is it?"

"She's been looking for her stepfather because she thinks he killed her mother."

"What the hell?"

"I know. Her mother died of a heart attack when Megan was eighteen. Her mother was an actress and made quite a lot under her name. Megan's stepfather took everything that belonged to his wife and Megan's inheritance then disappeared."

I grit my teeth when I think of what she must have gone through.

Levi pulls in a breath. "A friend of hers hired Gibbs to find her stepfather."

"Gibbs?" I raise my brows. That's a big name to know in our world.

"Megan's friend is married to James Marchesi."

That's interesting. His family isn't part of the alliance but is no less influential.

"I'm surprised they didn't step in to help her if Megan is friends with them."

"They don't know what happened to Hunter and are currently in Italy. I went through Megan's phone records from an old phone and looked over her text messages. It seems she fell out with her friend over Hunter. Her friend tried to warn her about him, but Megan didn't listen."

I understand now.

"Gibbs wasn't able to find Megan's stepfather, but I think I can."

"Really?"

"I have a few things I know Gibbs wouldn't try and I have my ways."

"Okay. Let's get this done." Everything else will have to wait.

Including me.

12

MEGAN

My nerves spike as Knox and I pull up outside Bill's shop.

I'm terrified of this confrontation and don't know what to expect.

"Hey." Knox brushes his hand over mine. The gentle touch soothes me and I'm reminded that I'm safe. "Don't be afraid."

"I'm trying not to be." I keep replaying last night over and over in my mind. Each time I do, it drains me.

"I'm not going to let anything happen to you."

"Thank you." I can't stop saying those words.

"Come, let's get this done." Knox's smile brightens and I summon courage.

We get out of his car and people look as we proceed up the path. When a man does a u-turn at the sight of Knox with the fear of God on his face, I feel safer.

As we walk into Bill's shop, the men inside look like they're going to shit themselves. One of them reaches for the phone but freezes when Knox takes out his gun and aims it at him.

"Don't even fucking think about picking up that phone." Knox's voice echoes around the room. "Is Bill in his office?"

"Yes." The guy nods.

"Perfect."

Taking my arm, Knox keeps me close and shields me with his body while we make our way to Bill's office.

When we get there, Knox doesn't bother to knock. He just kicks the door in, startling Bill, who is sitting behind his desk, counting out his money.

Terror fills every inch of his face when he sees Knox. Then his terror is replaced with regret, which deepens when his eyes dart to me.

"Bill Rodriguez, look at you. How you been?" Knox's voice is silky smooth and casual as if he's greeting someone in passing on a leisurely Sunday walk in the park.

"Knox, I... um. Well... I've just been here." Bill is stuttering.

My God in heaven, I never thought I'd live to see the day when Big Bad Bill looks like he's ready to shit himself.

"Now I heard my girl here was nearly kidnapped last night by your guys."

Bill's dark brows fly into his hairline. "Your girl?"

His girl?

Even I have to look at Knox too as raw surprise wracks my brain.

"My girl." He doesn't look at me as he gives the confirmation, but I notice how easily he speaks. The gesture touches my heart with that warmth of comfort I haven't felt in a long time.

"I didn't know she was yours." Bill rests a trembling hand on his desk.

"That's no excuse." Knox waves his gun toward Bill. "So I'm not sure you should get to live."

"What do you want?" Bill stutters, his gaze unwavering.

"You're going to give back every motherfucking cent that you took from her."

My eyes bulge so wide I fear they might pop out of my head. This was what sorting Bill out meant. Giving me back all the money that I paid. My breathing slows as retribution fills me and I reflect on the injustice I've suffered at the hands of this man.

Bill shakes his head and the tremor in his hands infects the rest of his body. "I have other people tied up in that money."

Knox issues him with a ruthless grin. "You mean like Sergei?"

Bill's dark skin pales at the mention of that name.

I have no idea who Sergei is, but if hearing his name can produce such an effect in Bill, I can only assume he must be someone more dangerous. Another man I shouldn't know about.

"Who is that?" I ask, finding my voice.

"Sergei is the Russian mafia leader Bill works for." Knox switches his gaze from Bill to me and the hardness in his eyes fades momentarily, revealing a glimpse of the compassionate side of him I've grown used to. "They were going to sell you on the human market as a sex slave then sell your organs when there was no more use for you."

Sheer black fright races over my body and I turn back to Bill. Last night made it clear my debt would never be repaid but hearing this...

Jesus. What a fucking asshole. Bill was going to sell me. *Sell* me and my organs. *My God.* How evil can one person be?

But this is my fault again. My fault for getting mixed up with Hunter.

"You fucking bastard." The words fly out of my mouth as if they have a life of their own. "I hope you rot in hell."

"Oh, he will. Rest assured." Knox's voice takes on a sing-song edge. "Bill, I suggest you do as I say. Pay her the money, or you're dead. You and I both know Hunter forged Megan's signature. You personally oversee all contracts. So you would have known she didn't sign anything because you were with Hunter when he set everything up."

What a despicable man. I remember how I begged him not to involve me in this. I pleaded with him, telling him there had been a terrible mistake, but he wouldn't listen. Of course not, because he saw me as a means to getting his repayment.

Bill's gaze flicks to mine for a moment, but then he returns his focus to Knox, probably thinking it's not wise to look away from him.

"Pay the fuck up. Now. Or this will be your last moment on earth." Knox cocks the hammer on his gun.

"I'll pay." Bill nods quickly, his head bobbing like it's attached to a bouncy spring.

Knox walks over to Bill as he starts tapping away at the keyboard of his computer.

Within two minutes, Bill announces he's repaid me all the money he took and didn't cash the check from yesterday.

"You forgot the interest." Knox taps the end of his gun to Bill's head.

I'm shocked enough as it is I'm getting my money back, but having interest as well makes me feel more redeemed.

"I think thirty percent interest sounds reasonable." A low chuckle rumbles in Knox's chest.

Bill clicks on the keyboard without argument, but the beads of sweat running down his horrid face shows his inner turmoil. "It's done. She has her money with interest."

Knox lowers his gun and dips his head. "Wonderful, now don't you ever fuck with me and mine again. Do it and you're dead. From this day onwards, you will forget you know Megan Porter. You will erase her name and details from your system and you will never see her again. Cross me, and I'll shoot your dick off, then feed it to you before I kill your ass. Capisce?"

"Capisce."

"Good."

Knox returns to me, slips an arm around my trembling shoulders and shepherds me back to the car. The realization of my freedom hits as we get in and tears stream down my cheeks.

Knox brushes his finger over my cheeks and cups my face. The warmth and comfort of his touch moves me into his arms and tears flow from my eyes like a river that's just broken through a dam.

"Thank you so much. You have no idea what I've been through and how scared I've been."

Knox pulls away a little so he can stare at me. "You are more than welcome."

"He was going to sell me, Knox." I sound raspy, choked with my tears. "Me."

He nods.

After what happened last night, I knew they would do their checks on me, but I never expected that type of shit to be unearthed. I was way in over my head and I didn't even know. I feel so foolish to think I had a handle on things. God knows what other dirty shit Knox and the others must have found on Hunter. I could see on their faces there was more.

"I'm sorry, baby." Knox dries my tears.

"I just can't believe you were able to get Bill to give me all that money back with interest and agree to leave me alone."

He looks a little uncomfortable. "Megan...the guys and I aren't that much dangerous from people like Bill. You need to know that. I think you do, right?"

"Yes, I know."

"Cristiano comes from a very influential family. My family and Levi's have always worked for the Riveras. No one wants to fuck with us because they know it means death if they do. That's how I was able to do what I did."

"I don't care who you are or how dangerous. I'm grateful to you. If you guys didn't help me, I don't know what would have happened to me by now."

"We protect what's ours," Knox mutters, resting his heavy hand on mine.

"I'm yours?" I manage a smile.

"I think you already knew that."

A surge of happiness fills me and I lean forward to kiss him, losing myself in his kissable lips.

He pulls out of the kiss and gives me a sexy smile. "How about we finish that later?"

"We better."

"Oh, we will. Now let's get the fuck out of here."

He guns the engine and as we speed down the road, I think of how grateful I am to each of my guys.

My guys...

How can they all feel like mine?

They do though and I know exactly how to repay them for what they did for me.

When Knox takes me back to Cristiano's house and I see him standing in the doorway between the kitchen and the living room, I rush into his arms.

"Thank you so much for everything," I tell him.

"You don't have to thank me." His heartbeat speeds up against my ear.

"Of course I do." I look up at him, stand on my toes and kiss him. "I feel safe again."

"That's all I wanted." He gives me a reassuring look before resting his hands on my shoulders. "We were able to take care of everything so you can get on with your life without the worry about anyone else linked to Hunter messing with you."

My hands fly up to my cheeks. "Oh my God, really?"

"Yes."

The nightmare is finally over.

I don't have to see Bill or his goons again or worry about anyone else coming after me. The only bitterness left to cope with is Hunter's duplicity and deception.

"I am indebted to you forever."

He chuckles. "No, you aren't."

"Don't I get a hug too?" Levi's voice booms from across the room.

I lift my head and see him with a sexy smirk on his face.

Leaving Cristiano's arms, I hug Levi and he laughs.

I look at each of them—my three knights in shining armor.

Cristiano comes closer. "I know I speak for all of us when I say you mean a lot to us."

They all nod respectfully, agreeing.

"You all mean a lot to me too. I meant it when I said I like you all. And I don't care how weird that sounds."

They look at each other and smile.

"In case you didn't notice, we're a little bit of an anomaly. We like weird." Cristiano grins.

"Good, because I'm going to accept your offer. I'll marry you and do whatever you need me to, but I don't want the money."

His brows furrow. "Megan, that's not why we did this for you."

"I know. But I can't ever really pay you back for getting me out of this mess. Marriage is a big deal, but I want to help you."

He takes my hand into his. "If you do this for me, you have to take the money. There's no negotiation otherwise. I mean it. If you insist, then there is no offer."

I think about it for a moment and nod. "Okay. Whatever it takes. I'll do it."

"Are you sure about this?"

"I am extremely sure."

"Then thank you."

"I'm happy to help."

Levi clears his throat and I look at him.

"I don't mean to change the subject, but while we're discussing serious matters, there's something I need to bring up."

"What?" I ask, curiosity spiking my nerves again.

"While I was looking into things, I saw you were trying to find your stepfather."

Any mention of that man jars me. "Yes. I am."

"I'm aware of what you're accusing him of and I'm going to help you."

My mouth drops. "You think you can find him?"

"I will do my best. If I can't find him, it means he's dead."

"Oh my gosh. Finding him would give me so much justice. I know he killed my mother."

"Then, as long as he's alive, I will deliver you justice."

13

MEGAN

Cristiano walks into the living room with two mugs of coffee. Although steam wafts out of the mugs, the shirtless, god-like man carrying them is hotter than sin.

I watch him set the coffee down on the table and resist the urge to drool at the sight of the perfect muscles lining his abs under his tattoos.

It's morning again and one of the best Sundays I've had for as long as I can remember. Since last night was the first I slept with the guys outside the club, my good spell began from then, and it's about to continue.

Knox and Levi will be back later. Until then, I have Cristiano.

It's time to talk about our arrangement, but that doesn't mean I can't appreciate how gorgeous he is.

He sits opposite me and runs a hand through his already ruffled just-got-out-of-bed sexy hair. The simple action makes him look sexier.

"You're giving me that look again." He smirks.

"Because you're sexy as hell and I can't help myself."

"Now you know how I feel." He taps the inside of my thigh and lowers to plant a kiss there. "I can't help myself too."

Instantly I want him inside me again. I want to go back to his bed and have him pounding into me hard while I wrap my legs around his waist.

I run my hand through his hair and stare down at him, looking past the hard exterior of the soon-to-be mafia boss.

"What will it be like when you become don of your family?"

He straightens and moves over to sit next to me. "I guess it's time to talk about that."

"Yeah."

"I wanted to give you a day to think properly because yesterday was so hectic. I didn't want your gratitude over-powering your decision."

"It hasn't. I still want to go through with it."

"How are you feeling though about it? You were married only months ago and you lost your husband."

"I don't know how I feel. I'm mostly numb, but that's it. I can get over numbness. I don't care about anything else. I don't have anyone I care about around me to factor in." Of course, I'm thinking about Paige. The truth is I'm all alone. So I can do what I want. "I'll do it because it helps you."

"You're helping me out in ways I can't describe."

"Then I'm glad to help."

He pulls in a deep breath. "The first hurdle we need to jump over is meeting my immediate family. We have dinner with them in ten days."

"What's your family like?"

"They're great if they like you, and they will. We just have to make everything believable. The first lie we'll tell is that your name is Evelina."

I raise my brows. "Evelina?"

"Yes. I made you up last year when my grandfather wanted to marry me off."

"Oh, I see."

"Don't worry. I'll bring you up to speed with everything, so you know what to say. We won't have many family gatherings, so you'll only have to remember you're Evelina a handful of times a year."

"That sounds doable." But nerve-wracking. I pray I don't slip up.

"I hope so. We just need to keep up the charade for three years, and that's it."

"I'm guessing you never want to get married and stay married?"

He brushes a wisp of hair from my face. "All I know is I don't like anyone forcing me to do anything. That's what my grandfather is doing. As to whether marriage is for me, well... I don't know. Maybe I'll know one day."

"Me too." Clearly, it was all wrong for me.

"I'm sorry about Hunter."

"Thank you. He just really blindsided me." I don't even want to think about that man ever again, so it's best we change the subject. "What happens after the dinner?"

"Italy in a little over four weeks. We'll be going there for my grandfather's birthday and to meet the rest of the family."

"Wow. Italy."

"You sound like you've been there." His eyes sparkle.

"I have. I was there for my best friend's wedding." And now I'm thinking about Paige again.

"Best friend?"

"She was. We fell out over Hunter. She saw straight through him and tried to warn me. I don't know why I didn't listen. She's in Italy now with her husband." Come to think of it, maybe Cristiano might know James. I wouldn't be surprised because earlier, Levi mentioned Gibbs. I'm sure an explanation of who introduced me to him would have come up.

"Do you want to make up with your friend?"

"I do. I'd love nothing more."

"Then, when we go to Italy, I think you should see her."

Could I?

I'm so embarrassed, but maybe fixing things with Paige is one more thing I can do sooner rather than later.

"Maybe I will."

"I think you should."

I smile. "It would be great to see her."

"I'm sure it would. Besides, I'd like to know you have a friend when I'm away. Or when you're away."

"Me?" I grin.

"You can go back to your training in L.A., Megan." He nods and my heart swells. Going back to college felt so far away from my reach that I thought it would never happen again. "You can go back whenever you want and set up your practice when the time comes. I travel a lot, but I'll also be here a lot more that I'm taking things over. That doesn't affect you. You'll have your own life and I'll support you whatever you do."

"Thank you. I can't believe this is even possible for me."

"Believe it because it is. Of course, I also want you to move in with me straightaway." His eyes drop to my breasts. "I'll send someone to get your things tomorrow."

I laugh. "You're just going to move me in."

"Yes. Are you complaining?"

Hell no, Cristiano lives in an eight-bed mansion with an Olympic-sized pool, tennis court and a garage that holds twenty cars that nearly cost the same as an average house. "I have no complaints at all."

I do have one more question on my mind that I think I already know the answer to, but I want to ask, so I'm sure. "What about the guys? Do we stop um... fooling around?"

"No, that's why you're perfect for this." He searches my eyes. "Unless you want—"

"No," I cut in. "I don't want to stop."

"Good."

"The four of us work for me. It's nice."

"I'm glad to hear that. You know what else is nice?" He looks over my body with wild seduction.

"What?"

"You riding my face with your tight little pussy. I think we need to go back to bed."

"I like that idea."

"Then come here, baby." He scoops me up and kisses me hungrily while he carries me upstairs.

This is like a dream and he's everything I've ever wanted.

I slip away and get lost in him easily, but part of me holds on to reality, remembering this is just a business arrangement.

I can't fall for him, or Levi, or Knox.

Cristiano is doing this because he wants control of his situation and as nice as this is with us, I'm a means to an end.

We have this fascination with each other and I have this thing going on with the group.

However, there will come a time when the sexual haze fades.

There will be an end and I just hope my heart can handle it.

It's going to be hard keeping control of my feelings when they've already captured my soul.

14

LEVI

"Wow." Megan's bright eyes widen with fascination as she steps into my apartment.

She has the same look most people have when they first come to my not-so-humble place of abode.

I don't have a flashy mansion like Cristiano, but I have an equally ostentatious luxury penthouse apartment in the heart of the city. It has everything from a private pool, terrace, garden, and best of all, the view. I've always been a city boy. Even when I'm in Italy, I prefer the fast pace life-style to the idyllic ambiance of the countryside. But maybe that's because of the way my parents raised me.

They were always away, and since I hated the silence of being alone, I sought anything with life and energy for comfort. That led me here.

Megan floats into the apartment like the angel she is and looks around at the less is more contemporary décor I have going on.

"I love it." She smiles, twirling around.

It's been a few days since the incident and she looks much better. I like seeing her like this. I know everything isn't okay and it will be a long time before it is, but she looks happier. That works perfectly because tonight is my night to have her.

This is the start of our arrangement. Cristiano, Knox and I spoke a few days ago. We came up with a plan on how we were going to share this perfect woman who has managed to work some kind of magic on us to make us contemplate a relationship with her.

It's as crazy as can be and way outside what we've ever done. Being at the Dark Odyssey and other sex clubs when we're traveling is different. This is taking the fantasy into the real world. I don't know how it will work, especially with this upcoming marriage, but I know we'll make it work the same way we do with everything else.

For now, she'll stay with Cristiano most of the time because we don't want anyone getting suspicious. Knox and I will then have her for a day each per week. We might be able to fit in two days sometimes. It won't matter anyway because we'll see her at Cristiano's place. These moments are just private and special.

Tonight was supposed to be Knox's night with her before the two of us head out to L.A., but we swapped because I know Megan is eager to talk about her stepfather. He is a subject we haven't spoken about since I first mentioned the possibility of finding him. It's early days yet, so I don't have any news, but I'm working on getting something. Over the last few days, it crossed my mind that her stepfather could only have disappeared the way he did if he knew the right people. People who could hide him so well it's like he never existed. It's people like that I've started looking into.

Her light laughter pulls me from my thoughts.

"Your apartment is like a cross between Bruce Wayne's mansion and Iron man's, whatever you call his place." Her eyes sparkle.

"I've heard that before." I chuckle. "But Cristiano is more Bruce Wayne than me. All he's missing is an Alfred. He does have staff, though."

"I agree."

"Come, let's go sit by the pool." I slip my arm around her waist and pull her closer. She looks tiny next to me, but when she puts her arm around me, we fit. "Maybe we can go for a swim."

"I like that. Means I get to look at you shirtless."

I love the way she speaks her mind. "Oh, I'm a firm believer in swimming naked. You know what that means for you too." I give her ass a firm squeeze and lower to crush my lips to hers.

We kiss for a few moments and I enjoy tasting her. When I pull away, I take her hand and lead her into the hallway.

I grab a bottle of Merlot and two long-stemmed glasses, then take her out to the pool. We sit side by side at the pool-side, watching the waning sun and I pour her a glass of wine. When I hand it to her, I note that hope-filled look in her eyes again and I know she's thinking about her stepfather.

I kiss the top of her nose and set the bottle down.

"I'm working on finding him, Megan," I say as if I'm continuing a conversation we've already been having.

My lips part and she sets her glass down next to the bottle. "How did you know I was thinking about him?"

"I just do."

She sighs, hugging her knees into her chest, instantly

appearing smaller and more girl-like. It's as if she's giving the strong woman we've seen in her over the last few weeks a break. What I'm seeing seems like a glimpse into her most vulnerable side.

I know what it feels like to be vulnerable. It's the worst kind of curse for a strong person.

"I don't know how you will find my stepfather." She stares deeply at me. "But I'm grateful you want to help me. Life has been tough for a long time."

"I can imagine. What made you suspect him, Megan?"

"I knew in my heart and when he disappeared with everything my mother owned, I knew I was right. The police didn't really help even though they tried to find him. Before Gibbs, I had a lawyer investigating, but I ran out of money." She pauses for a beat. "When my mother married my stepfather, I sensed he was after her money. They met on the set of one of her tv shows. He moved in after dating her for a few weeks. Then they got married months later. Mom thought he was everything, but he was a fucking asshole. If she ever knew what he was like she..."

Her voice trails off and I wonder if there was more her stepfather did to her that she doesn't want to talk about.

"Sometimes people can't see the truth when they're in love."

"Yes. And that applies to me too. I followed in my mother's footsteps when it came to Hunter. I guess maybe now I finally understand. She couldn't see my stepfather for what he was and I couldn't see behind the mask Hunter showed me. At least, thanks to you guys, I'm not dead."

I rest my hand on top of hers. "I think the situation with Hunter was different for you because you knew him back in high school. We don't expect people like that to screw with us."

"No, we don't." A faraway look comes into her eyes. "Everything still hurts, Levi. Time has passed and life has moved on, but I'm still in pain."

"Because you haven't had closure."

"No, I haven't. Even if I do get that, I'm not sure the pain will go away."

"It lessons, but you never really get over things like that."

She studies my face. "You sound like you're speaking from experience."

"I am."

"What happened to you?"

"When I was twelve, I watched my grandparents get killed. We were attacked on the beach in Sicily."

She sucks in a sharp breath. "Oh my God, Levi, that's awful."

"It was horrific. My grandfather just managed to get me to safety with my older cousin. We escaped on a motorcycle. I remember him getting shot and screaming for us to keep going. We did. Sometimes I regret that. At other times I remember how much my grandfather loved us and would have hated himself if he'd died knowing we did too."

"I think he would have. Were the killers ever found?"

I look away for a moment. Every time I tell this story, it hits me hard. Looking back at her, I reaffirm my thoughts on what I did during that time. "Yes. Years later, I found out it was my uncle who arranged it all." Those skills of mine revealed things I never thought possible about a man I trusted.

Her skin pales. "Your uncle?"

"Yes. My dear uncle found out my grandfather had

discovered his shady dealings and wrote him out of his will. The massacre was the only way he could have any claim to the family inheritance."

"That's beyond evil. He killed his parents."

"And countless others." Many of my cousins died that day and I could have died too.

"What happened to him?"

"I killed him." I say that with the same lack of emotion I felt when I shot my uncle in the head. That was mere moments after I ran my car into him. The bullet to the head was to ensure his death.

My grandparents were more like parents to me than my own. So my uncle was mine to kill. Especially since I knew my father wouldn't do it. My uncle was an asset to him who brought in all sorts of money that nearly rivaled the Riveras. Knowing the kind of bastard my father is, he would have found some excuse to keep my uncle alive. That's why I took matters into my own hands and ensured the rest of the family knew about his treachery so I wouldn't be punished for my actions.

I expected Megan to be fazed by my words, but she isn't. There's no ounce of judgment in her eyes. Instead, I see compassion and understanding.

"Did you feel better? People say revenge isn't real justice, but I don't know if I believe that. My mother was my everything. She was both mother and father to me. I... never knew my birth father. I watched her drop dead in front of me and my world ended. I knew even as I watched her die that my stepfather did something to her."

Her words seep into my heart and I find myself vowing to do all I can to make up for her loss.

"I promise you I won't stop looking for him."

The light comes back to her eyes. "I can't thank you enough."

"Come here." I take her hand and pull her onto my lap. We fall into a longing kiss and as my cock hardens, I just want to get lost in her.

"I need you," she whispers against my lips.

"Then I'm all yours."

15

CRISTIANO

My mother looks across the dining table at Megan and smiles with approval.

That's a win for me, but the biggest victory is my grandfather approves too.

This is the dinner meetup I was dreading. Instead of turning into a disaster, the night has been a success.

Seated around the Arthurian-style table is my mother, my grandparents, Lorenzo, Megan, and me.

Lorenzo is the only person here who hasn't looked happy to see Megan. The asshole has sat in his chair looking stiffer than board left to dry out in the sun for far too long. He was expecting me to fuck up tonight and I nearly did.

Every time Megan is referred to as Evelina, I recall how closely I fucked up.

Judging from the proud look on my grandfather's face as he listens to Megan talk about her work with UNICEF, I know I have this in the bag and the empire at my fingertips.

It has my name on it and the bonus is her—Megan Porter.

She makes this scheme believable because it's clear to

everyone around us that I want her. I can't stop looking at her, and it's obvious when I'm thinking about her.

I can't stop my heart from leaping whenever she smiles at me any more than I can calm the hardening in my cock, or the need to bend her over the table and fuck her.

Tonight she looks beautiful in a navy sleeveless dress which hugs and caresses her body in all the ways I want to. It's the kind of dress to make a man go crazy.

I've never met a woman who could make me lose control the way she does.

It's unnerving because we've only known each other for a little over a month.

So how can I feel this way?

Maybe she just has that magic about her because I can tell my family loves her. They don't love easily. You have to work hard to earn it.

I suppose if Megan were working tonight to earn their love, she would have deserved every ounce of admiration my family has shown her.

She played the natural and took our made-up story to award-winning romance status.

Her beautiful autumn eyes glistened when she told them the story of how we met at the coffeehouse in the city and how I asked her out on our first date when I fixed her car. Then her cheeks flushed a vibrant color when she told everyone how I proposed.

As Megan showed off the oval-cut diamond engagement ring I gave her last week, my grandmother teared up. The ring looks similar to hers, so I knew what I was doing when I bought it.

"So, when can we start wedding planning?" Grandfather directs the question at me and takes my grandmother's hand. "I would love for the wedding to be soon."

In any other family, he would seem abrupt and the suggestion inappropriate. But in our family, my grandfather is still the law and it doesn't matter what people think of him.

The question also isn't really a question. It's an order to get plans for this wedding together as soon as humanly possible.

"We're hoping to get married in six weeks." That's when I can sort everything out for the wedding I know he wants me to have.

"Six weeks is perfect," Mother says, brightening her already radiant smile.

"It will have to do," Grandfather concedes. "I trust you will be bringing Evelina to my birthday celebration in Italia."

"Yes." I glance at Megan.

"I can't wait to attend," Megan says in a voice sweeter than sugar.

I catch sight of the narrowed look Lorenzo gives her and I don't like it. All I want is for him to believe what I'm showing the world and back the fuck off, but I can see he's scrutinizing and trying to dissect us.

I think he suspects my relationship isn't real. Which means this motherfucker could stir shit if I don't take enough precautions to protect my plans.

I created a whole personality for Evelina and Levi did what he could to conceal Megan's real name and hide certain details about her so she can't be tracked.

Things are bulletproof, but Lorenzo is a man like me. We resort to desperate measures when we don't get what we want. I just have to make sure I'm one step ahead of him.

Grandfather raises his wine glass and looks at each person sitting around the table. "This is a good night. I only wish my son was here to see us all together celebrating this beautiful news." He nods at me with fervency. "My boy would be as proud of you as I am."

Uncontrollable guilt stabs at me. I know he's proud. My father would indeed be too. So I can't help feeling like I'm spitting in their faces to get what I want.

I just hope this plan doesn't blow up and cause any disappointment. I'm not the man to care about such things, but I do when it comes to my family.

Grandfather looks at Megan and reaches out to take her hand. She gives it to him and I can see she's as awed as I am.

"Welcome to the family, Evelina. I can see you make my grandson very happy just by how he looks at you."

"Thank you so much. I appreciate that a lot." She glances at me and smiles, her eyes twinkling.

Grandfather lifts his glass higher. "To family past, present, and future. And to Cristiano, the next don of this family."

That sounds like music to my ears.

This is really happening. We just need to be married now to make everything official then I don't have to worry anymore.

I raise my glass in appreciation and toast to the success I hope to gain when I take over the leadership. But when I look at Megan, I feel like I already have everything I want. As I study her face, her cheeks flush and the tenderness in her eyes suggests she feels the same way too.

The evening wears on and the women talk in the garden while I play pool with my grandfather and Lorenzo in the den. Lorenzo didn't know I could see the evil looks he cast my way as we played.

It's in plain sight at the end of the night when I have Megan on my arm and I'm saying my goodbyes to everyone.

The asshole comes up to us after my grandmother hugs Megan and walks away with my grandfather.

"Congratulations again." Lorenzo stares at me with sordid scrutiny stretching out his hand to shake mine. "Almost thought you wouldn't be able to pull this off."

I take his hand and give him my best confident smile, knowing exactly what he means. He looks from me to Megan, the suspicion in his eyes intensifying.

"Almost thought you made up, Evelina." He tilts his head to the side and those hawk eyes of his bore into me with added venom, like a poison-tipped spear.

Something inside me tightens. It's not my stomach or the tightening you experience when nerves hit you or you're worried about something. It's more like the tension you feel when things are about to slip out of your control and you have to hold everything together. Including your sanity.

"But as you can see, she's right here." I keep my tone measured on purpose to show him I'm not fazed, although I am.

"Indeed." He looks at Megan like he's still skeptical of her.

"Good to meet you, my dear." He takes her hand and brings it up to his lips to kiss her knuckles. The gesture toward another man's woman would be disrespectful if we were sticking to tradition, but he gets away with it because we've always treated him like family. "I'm sure you'll make an excellent addition to the Rivera family."

"Thank you. That's so sweet of you to say." Megan is a better woman than I give her credit for. I know she can sense he's fake as fuck, yet she still smiles graciously, showing him the same respect you'd give a priest.

"Enjoy the rest of your evening." Lorenzo tips his head and walks away.

Megan tugs on my arm and I look at her. Worry is evident on her face, but she masks it with a smile.

I brush my cheek over hers. "Come on, let's get out of here."

She nods and I take her hand. I don't let her go until we're in my car.

Neither of us speaks until we're a few miles away from my Grandfather's house.

"I really hope I didn't mess up tonight." Megan gives me a tentative stare.

I reach across and rest my hand on her thigh. "You did amazing."

"But Lorenzo was weird."

"I know. Don't worry about him."

"I can see you're worried."

I give her hand a gentle squeeze. "Don't worry about me."

"But I do."

"You can make me feel better when we get home." That makes her smile.

"Maybe I can get a head start." Her perfectly manicured fingers run over the zipper of my pants and she strokes my dick.

"Do you feel better?" She massages the growing bulge and strokes me harder when I groan, giving her an answer to her question.

"Much."

"Good, there will be more where that came from when we get back." She giggles.

With that promise, I accelerate and get home in record time. The moment I park up on the drive, I lift her out of the car and lay her over the hood. Then I fuck her right there.

I'm not usually selfish, but tonight I can't help but be grateful I have Megan all to myself. She's all mine too for the next few days while Knox and Levi are on business trips.

I keep her with me pretty much all the time and we fuck every chance we get like we're possessed.

It's only when I'm away days later that I realize the truth of why I feel so complete when I'm with her.

It's because I'm in love with her.

Nothing is clearer or truer. I love her, and I'm looking forward to making her my wife.

16

MEGAN

"Your safe word is red." Levi's sensual lips smooth over mine as he tightens the straw-colored rope binding my wrists above my head.

I'm naked and attached to the rope hanging from the beam in the ceiling of the sex dungeon.

Of course, like everything at The Dark Odyssey, the room is made with that flair of eccentricity. It has everything we need for the wild BDSM night the guys have planned for me. There is an assortment of ropes, restraints, clit and nipple clamps, a St. Andrew's cross, lubricants and every sex toy known to man.

"Say it and we stop." Levi chuckles. "Understand, Goddess?"

"Yes, sir." That's what I'm supposed to call my guys tonight.

A pang of arousal goes straight to my pussy when he gives me a wicked smile that speaks of all the dirty things he's planning to do to me.

Knox and Cristiano wear the same devilish grins and my

entire body blushes with wildfire when they both crouch to lick my ass cheeks and fondle my pussy.

Cristiano's mood has improved since the dinner with his family two weeks ago, but I know he's still worried. I'm afraid too, because I know the façade we're trying to pull off is wrong. Although I fear the secret may be revealed someday, I'll continue to do my part.

I'd feel terrible if that were ever to happen because I like his family. They remind me of what I always hoped for when I got married. Hunter's family was nice, but his mother never really liked me from high school and she didn't like the fact that her son married me. I didn't care then and I truly don't give a fuck now.

I push her out of my mind as I slip back into this fantasy of me being devoured by three of the hottest men on earth.

At least in these moments, no matter what we're worried about, we can escape in each other.

The three of them. And me.

Being here to have fun with my guys is exhilarating. We arrived about fifteen minutes ago after spending the day together.

I'm always amazed at how everything has felt as natural with each of them as it would for people in a monogamous relationship. We created this amazing relationship where I would do anything for them and in turn, they'd give me the sun, moon, and every star in the galaxy if they could. I know they're spending a lot of time searching for my stepfather and it's going to be a task to find him. I accept they might never be successful but knowing they care so much about me means everything.

Now we're here and they have me at their mercy. They are my sexy, ruthless Doms and I'm their lucky Sub.

Cristiano places his hand against my stomach and runs his fingers across my skin. His touch feels so damn good. Like a potent dose of pleasure.

Everything is amplified when Knox and Levi join him and the three circle me like predators marking their prey.

"We plan to give you the hardest fuck you've ever had in your life," Knox stands before me and traces the outline of my jaw. "Are you ready for us?"

"I was born ready for you." I think I was. Every time I'm with them, I grow closer and closer. My body bows and molds to take them whenever they're inside me, as if I was destined to be theirs.

Cristiano is the first to plunge into me, taking me from behind. Knox and Levi alternate between kissing me and sucking my breasts.

Pleasure is amplified by the fact that I'm prevented from moving and all I can do is feel what they want to give me.

I slip into a pleasure coma as they take turns to fuck me. I'm hardly aware when they cut the ropes down and carry me over to the sofa so Knox and Levi can double penetrate me.

When it's Cristiano's turn to have me, he finishes inside me like always and I find myself wishing we could all be like this forever.

I'm woken by the softest touch on my cheek. It feels like a feather running over my skin.

I open my eyes to bright sunlight, disorientated until I see Levi's face looming over me.

I don't know when I fell asleep or when we left the club,

but we're in Cristiano's room back at his home.

"Hi." I reach out and touch Levi's face.

He lowers and gives me a gentle kiss. "Morning, sleepy head, or actually it's afternoon."

I gasp, sitting up instantly. *Afternoon?* No wonder it's so bright outside.

"My God. What time is it?"

"It's nearly one-thirty. I guess we wiped you out."

They certainly did. I slip my hand over my mouth to stop myself from laughing out loud.

"I'm wiped out in a good way."

"I was hoping you would say that." He smiles as radiantly at me as the warm sun kissing my skin, but the smile recedes as worry clouds his eyes. Instantly I know something's not right.

"Where are the others? Is… everything okay."

"It will be. After today I'm sure your life will be better. I just don't like taking you into the darker parts of my world."

I grimace, swallowing hard. "What do you mean, Levi?"

"I found your stepfather, Megan."

My breath catches and my brain flip-flops as I try to process his words. When I do, adrenaline races through my body, seizing my heart and lungs at the same time.

Levi found my stepfather.

He actually did it.

"You did it. You found him?" My voice comes out in a gentle hush that reminds me of the broken girl I was at eighteen who'd just lost her mother and knew she didn't die of natural causes. The solid walls of my world came crashing down all around me that day and I've been lost since. All because of that bastard—my so-called stepfather.

"Yes. He was hiding out in Mexico. I found him two days

ago, but I didn't want to say anything until my men had secured him. They did yesterday and arrived in Chicago earlier this morning."

I can't believe what he's saying to me or that it's real. "My God, Levi. I don't know how to thank you." I hug him and he rubs my back.

"Anything for you." He bows and a lock of his hair falls over his eye. "Knox and Cristiano are with your stepfather at one of the facilities where we question people. I decided to stay with you until they were ready to give the all-clear for you to see him. Cristiano called five minutes ago to do so."

At the thought of seeing my stepfather again, goosebumps line the back of my neck. I haven't seen him since before mom's funeral.

"Baby, are you ready to see him?"

"Yes." I've been ready to look that evil bastard in the eye for years and tell him I know what he did.

The building Levi referred to as 'one of their facilities' is an old warehouse by the docks. It looks like something you'd find in a nineties horror film and even has the eerie vibe to accompany the stiff atmosphere.

Levi leads me in, keeping his arm around my waist. I think he can see how much my legs are shaking, although my mind and spirit are willing to face my biggest demon.

"This way." Levi motions down a set of dark stairs and we take them.

At least the overhead lights snap on when the motion sensors catch our first steps. Having the light takes the edge off but does nothing to calm my racing heart.

KHARDINE GRAY & FAITH SUMMERS

We walk through a set of metal doors and then I see him. My stepfather, the great Samuel Richardson, is tied to a chair. He's covered in bluish-black bruises and blood. Despite that, he looks like he's had a good life and hasn't aged much since I last saw him.

Cristiano and Knox stand on either side of him. Both men have guns, but Cristiano is also holding a butcher knife at his side with blood dripping from it.

He glances at me as Levi and I stop a few paces away, then he lifts my dear stepfather's face with the edge of the knife to level his gaze with mine.

"Samuel, look at Megan. She's here." Cristiano speaks in a low voice. I've gotten to realize that the calm side of him is the most dangerous.

"Hello Samuel, long time no see." I never stopped dreaming of this day. So I know what to say despite my nerves.

"Long time, Princess."

Princess was what my mother used to call me. He was never welcome to the pet name.

I scowl at him. "Do not call me that."

For the two years he was married to my mother, I endured him calling me princess because of Mom. She never heard the times when he called me a little bitch because I wouldn't let him fuck me.

I never told anybody about that and I tried to make myself forget it ever happened. His disgusting propositions were constant and I was just grateful I could stand up to him. God knows how I would have managed if he'd come into my life when I was younger because I know I wouldn't have had the balls.

Still, I kept my silence partly because I was embarrassed.

The other part of me knew how badly it would have hurt my mother. Mom was so in love with him that her heart would have shattered to hear he wasn't the man she thought he was.

Now it doesn't matter.

"Why don't you tell Megan everything you told me about how her mother died." Cristiano's voice cuts into my thoughts.

Through the bruises marring Samuel's face, I take note of his apprehension.

When he stalls, Cristiano knees him in the gut. Samuel shouts in agony and coughs blood.

"Talk, or you'll die quicker." Knox gathers up Samuel's hair and yanks it so hard he rips out some of the strands.

"I'll talk." Samuel looks over at me and coughs again. "Your mother... didn't just have a heart attack."

"You killed her, didn't you?" I grit my teeth.

"Yes. It was a poison you can't detect unless you're looking for specific things. The coroner wouldn't have been able to pick it up, especially since I gave it to her in small doses."

"You bastard." I rush forward and throw a hard punch in his face. I hit him again and again until Levi pulls me off him.

"Tell her you're sorry," Cristiano orders. "She knows you don't mean it, but she needs to hear you say it."

I look at Cristiano, wondering how he knows.

And he's right. No apology on earth would appease me or compensate for my loss but hearing it means something.

"I'm sorry." Samuel says the words and I don't sense anything genuine in him. The only thing he's sorry about is that he got caught.

"I'm sorry too. I wish you never came into our lives. I hate you with everything inside me." My heart is racing so fast that I fear it will burst out of my chest and keep speeding for miles and miles and miles. I'm so worked up I can't calm myself.

On seeing the mess I'm fast becoming, Cristiano cocks his head to the side and signals to Levi. "Get her back home now, both of you."

Knox comes over to me and he and Levi take my arm on either side to lead me away.

Before I reach the stairs, I look back at my stepfather one last time.

Our eyes lock and I know I'll never see him again.

I contemplate what Cristiano will do with him, but when we get outside and one loud scream sounds all around us, I get my answer.

The silence which follows confirms my darkest thought. That my stepfather is dead.

Men like Cristiano Rivera don't leave you alive.

That visit was for me to get my apology and to say goodbye.

Goodbye, Samuel Richardson. Justice is served, Mom. An eye for an eye. Blood for blood.

Maybe I can find the strength to move on with my life now.

I think I can finally try.

It's nearly ten o'clock when Cristiano comes home.

As he walks into the living room where I've been watching TV with Levi and Knox, I notice he looks more like himself. He's changed into his usual dark clothes and is carrying a briefcase.

I should feel weird that Cristiano killed Samuel, but I don't.

I can see Cristiano is expecting me to feel some kind of fear when he looks at me, but I smile at him.

Levi and Knox stand when he comes closer. They took care of me, giving that added support. I suppose I needed it after what happened today.

"We're gonna head home tonight and give you some time to talk," Knox says.

"Cool, see you tomorrow." Cristiano gives him a reassuring pat on his shoulder, then sits next to me.

He drags in a deep breath when Levi and Knox leave and keeps his gaze riveted to mine.

"You okay?" He runs a finger over my thigh.

"I'm okay."

"Are you sure?"

"Yes. Thank you for slaying my demon."

"You are always welcome." He slips an arm around me and pulls me toward his chest. I rest against the hard wall savoring the sound of his heart beating against my ear. "How about a walk by the river? I think I need some peace and fresh air."

"That sounds perfect."

It does.

When we get up and he takes my hand, energy surges through me.

Cristiano and the guys didn't just slay one of my demons. They set my life back on track and I feel like a new person. One who can go anywhere from here.

17

KNOX

The sultry, sexy sounds of Megan's moans fill the living room when I walk in.

She's been a new woman since we dealt with her stepfather.

My eyes land on her on her hands and knees on the floor while Levi pounds into her from behind. He's fucking her mercilessly like he can't get enough.

She's supposed to be all mine today because it's my day off, but the greedy asshole came over on his lunch break. That was two hours ago and he doesn't look like he has plans to leave any time soon.

That's fine because I don't plan to let him have all the fun. The two of them look at me and smile when I sit in the armchair and watch.

I'm not sure which of us enjoys watching people fucking more. I know I have an unhealthy fascination with it. Way back when we were curious boys, I was also the one to come up with the idea of sharing. I was fifteen and should have had my head in my books but had all sorts of fucked up things on my mind.

It was a shocker because I'm the one with the church-going family. I'm also the one with parents who were the least dysfunctional. Cristiano's parents come in a very close second but were overly strict when we were younger.

It wasn't until we were sixteen that we first shared a girl. We've been sharing ever since.

As Levi hammers harder into Megan and the sound of sex fills the room, she comes. This is the part where I think I'm supposed to get jealous because she came on his dick and I wanted her on mine. But I don't feel anything close to jealousy. Neither of us ever do.

It wouldn't make sense to people on the outside, but It does for us.

We knew our unconventional relationship would get complicated and feel awkward at times. However, when we're together, things feel too right to be wrong or awkward.

Like now, I love watching the pleasure on Megan's face as she yields to desire.

It's beautiful. So beautiful, I move closer and touch her face.

I kiss her and play with her breasts, falling into the rhythm of Levi's thrusts as our tongues tangle.

I was going to wait for him to finish before I had my share of her, but fuck it. I can't wait. Nothing about this woman has been good for my already non-existent patience. She's too damn sexy.

Moreover, things will be tense next week when we're in Italy. We'll be around Cristiano's family, which means we'll have to be extra careful.

Weeks ago, Cristiano told me about Lorenzo's suspicions

about his relationship with Megan. People like Lorenzo have also suspected us of sharing women. While it might be okay under other circumstances, if anyone finds out we're sharing here, it would be one more thing to jeopardize the plan. Cristiano's grandfather would not be okay with it.

So in moments like these, we can enjoy her in whatever ways we want.

As I pull out of the kiss and take off my clothes, she watches me with a pretty smile.

"My turn now," I declare, bumping fists with Levi. "Time to switch out."

Levi pulls out of Megan and gives her ass a gentle smack. "I warmed her up for you."

She laughs. "I'm always ready for you."

"Good, because I'm going to fuck your brains out." I grab her, turn her ass to me and slam my already hard dick into her dripping wet pussy. She feels too good to go slow, so I fuck her hard. She knows how I like it, so she's used to me.

Sexy moans fall from her lips once more, rippling between Levi and me.

He watches me now fucking our girl and I know he can see beyond my usually guarded exterior the same way I can with him. He knows I crossed the line weeks ago and fell for her nearly the same time he did.

What I wonder is how we'll let her go when the three years are up.

Is it a bad thing that I want to keep her and make her ours forever?

~

Levi doesn't leave that night. We tag team Megan and spend the time in bed.

I don't get her entirely to myself until the next evening when I take her to dinner at a quaint little French restaurant on the other side of town.

I brought her here because it's far away from where most people in our circle travel. It's also discreet.

We spend hours talking and I love listening to her even if I don't get some of her music or what she loves about helping people talk through their problems.

"You have to listen to my Goo Goo Dolls album when we get back." She bubbles and her ponytail bounces.

I chuckle at the thought of me listening to music like that. "Baby, can you really see me listening to Goo Goo Dolls?"

"Yes, you'll love it."

I reach for her hand, but just as I'm about to take it, something catches my attention. I look to my left and find myself staring at Lorenzo standing on the second-floor balcony.

My hand stills on the table and my insides twist as our eyes lock and neither of us looks away.

What the fuck is he doing here?

If memory serves me correctly, Lorenzo hates the French as much as he hates their food. Since I already know about his suspicions, I don't think this is some chance meeting. My gut is telling me he's here because he's watching us.

And he wants me to know it. That's why the motherfucker has emerged from the shadows like a bad dream, eager to make his presence known.

Quickly I mull over what I did with Megan. I never kissed her, and I didn't touch her too much, but I know we look like we're on a date. Because we are.

Megan continues her chatter, oblivious to Lorenzo.

KHARDINE GRAY & FAITH SUMMERS

I look away from him and back at her, but out of the corner of my eye, I notice when he moves from where he stood. A quick look back confirms he's not there anymore.

"Baby, let's get out of here and listen to some of that music." I tap the back of her hand and grin.

"I'd love that. Let me just run to the ladies quickly. Then I'll be ready to go."

I nod and she saunters away.

I pay the bill and wait by the archway near the ladies bathrooms, hoping Megan hurries so we can leave soon.

My hopes die when Lorenzo approaches me with an uncanny smile plastered on his wrinkly face.

Shit. He's smiling. That's never good.

"Buona serata." He dips his head. "Fancy seeing you here."

"I was going to say the same thing about you. What are you doing here, Lorenzo?" It's best not to waste time with small talk about shit and pleasantries.

"Meeting a client."

"Oh really?"

"Yes, they just left."

He's lying. I know he is. This isn't the type of place *he'd* meet clients. Not that there's anything wrong with this restaurant. It's just not his scene. His ass is far too pompous.

"I hope things went well." I decide to play along.

"Always." His shit-eating grin grows and the suspicion I feared drips from his piercing stare. "I see you've been taking care of Cristiano's fiancée quite well."

"He has a meeting, so I was keeping her company."

"She's fortunate." He inclines his head and runs a hand over his gray beard. "With you guys around, I'm sure she'll never be bored."

"No, she won't."

"Well, have a nice night. See you in Italy."

I dip my head and keep my eyes on him as he walks away. When he goes through the door, I get out my phone and call Cristiano. He answers on the first ring.

"What's going on?"

"We have a problem. Lorenzo is watching us."

18

MEGAN

I started having fun the moment we arrived in Italy.

We got here two days ahead of schedule to do some sightseeing.

The guys took me everywhere, from the Vatican and Trevi Fountain in Rome to Venice, Verona, and Tuscany.

We finally settled down in Sicily, where I met the rest of Cristiano's huge, huge, huge family, and it was beautiful. They had a barbeque on the beach and welcomed me with open arms.

It was terrific to meet them all, but just like when I first met his grandparents and mother, guilt and nerves crept in every time people called me Evelina.

After a long day spent with Cristiano's mother and grandparents, I'm on the beach again with the guys. This time we're having a bonfire.

They've been teaching me Italian while we roast marshmallows under the star-speckled sky.

"I sound terrible." I giggle. "Like a mule giving birth."

The guys try not to laugh but fail.

"Baby, learning a new language comes with time." Cristiano pulls me into his lap and I slip my arm around his neck.

"But I still sound like a mule giving birth."

"Be that as it may, you sound like a very sexy mule giving birth," Levi says, raising a finger as if he's making an important point.

I throw a marshmallow at him and he catches it with his mouth.

Knox laughs, throwing more marshmallows at Levi, which he tries to catch too.

Cristiano shakes his head at them. "You guys never change."

"There's no need to." Levi high-fives Knox.

Cristiano grins and looks at me. "I hope you can get used to this."

"I already am, and I love it." I don't think I've ever said anything more truthful.

"Good to hear." He strokes my cheek. "Goddess, you should go see your friend over the next few days. You'll feel better for it."

In the moonlight, his blue eyes capture mine and I nod. I've been thinking about Paige even more since we got here. I want to see her. I'm just worried she won't want to see me.

"I'm gonna see her and hope for the best."

"If she's anything like what you've told us, I'm sure things will be fine," Knox says and Levi nods, agreeing.

"I hope so."

Cristiano presses his cheek to mine and it feels so good. Everything feels amazing and I can't imagine my life any other way.

Me with Cristiano, Levi, and Knox.

I know we have to be careful when we're together like this, but these are my favorite moments because I'm absolutely head over heels in love with all three of them.

"I think it's time we play with you."

"Me too."

19

CRISTIANO

I take a drag on my cigar and blow a ring of smoke through the opened window.

I'm in one of the private cottages by the lake. From where I am, I can see the castle-like structure of the château that's been in my family for over a hundred years. Beyond that is the beach.

The picturesque scenery enchants me the same way it did when I was a child. I remember the time I spent here with my parents and all the memories that will stay with me forever.

The beautiful maiden asleep on my bed provides a different sort of enchantment. One I never expected from anybody.

She was always beautiful, but there's something epic about being able to see inner beauty and noticing when it overwhelms everything about the external.

Over the last few days, I've found myself thinking about the future with her and the guys. Instead of being a business transaction, my relationship with her feels real to me.

My phone buzzes in my back pocket, so I put out my cigar and make my way out of the room to answer the call.

I furrow my brows when I see it's my grandfather. He never calls me this early unless something is wrong.

"Buongiorno, Grandfather."

There's a pause for a beat then he sighs with what sounds like frustration. "Cristiano, I need you to come to my office. Bring Evelina with you. And the guys."

There's an edge to his voice that pulls at my insides.

Something is wrong.

I can feel it, hear it in his voice, and sense it spiking my nerves.

He summons me all the time, so that's no cause to worry. But why would he need to see Megan and the guys?

Fuck. I think he knows about us. I don't know how because I've been extremely careful since we got here, but something tells me he knows the truth.

"Sure. I'll be there in about ten minutes."

Ten minutes later, the four of us walk into my grandfather's office. I know my fears are correct when I see Lorenzo inside, standing by the desk.

The disappointment on my grandfather's face is even more confirmation.

"Hello, Grandfather. What's going on?"

"Play the recording," he says to Lorenzo instead of answering me.

Lorenzo holds out a remote control toward the widescreen monitor on the wall and when he clicks the button, the image of the four of us together having sex with Megan comes on.

My heart stops and my mouth opens as if I'm going to say

something. Except nothing comes out. I don't know what I would say or what explanation I would give.

Megan is sandwiched between Knox and Levi while the two of them are fucking her. I'm kissing her, then I swap places with Knox and plunge into her ass.

The fucking footage is from last night. We've been careful with our relationship, but it wouldn't have mattered because this is a recording from inside the bedroom. Lorenzo, the motherfucking prick, put cameras in my room and I fell right in his fucking trap. He was just waiting for us to slip up.

Grandfather takes the remote from Lorenzo and switches off the recording. His eyes burn like hot coals when he looks back at me.

"Grandfather I—"

"No. No more lies. That is just the tip of the shit." He looks away from me and focuses on Lorenzo. "Why don't you tell me everything you found on my grandson's supposed fiancée."

"With pleasure, my friend." Lorenzo's voice is full of amplified compassion. It's only contrasted with the victory in his eyes when he looks at me. "It turns out there was never any Evelina. This woman's real name is Megan Porter."

"I can explain," I attempt, but Grandfather holds up his hand.

"Don't you say a fucking word. Continue, please, Lorenzo."

"Certainly. Megan's landlord was kind enough to give me details about her and her late husband, Hunter Reid. Then I received further information from Bill Rodriguez, who told me Megan was working at the Dark Odyssey. It seems that Cristiano only met her a few months ago. There's no evidence of contact before that, like we've been led to believe or that she's a humanitarian worker. I also found over a million dollars paid into her account from Cristiano. Clearly, their relationship was all fake and fabricated to get the business and that money was to pay her off." The sneer he issues me cuts me deep because I landed myself in this mess.

Levi did all he could to cover certain things, but there are some things that can't be covered up. Once Lorenzo found out Megan's name from wherever the hell he did, he found all those parts too. Clearly, he started investigating me from the night of the dinner and worked overtime to dig for the truth.

"Grandfather, please let me talk."

"Okay, Cristiano, tell me you didn't pay this woman to be your fiancée." He stands and balls his hands into fists by his sides. "Tell me that's not you and your friends on that video fucking her. Tell me you didn't lie to get the business. Go on, do it."

My body goes rigid and I can't look away from his overbearing gaze.

"It's true. I did all those things," I answer and Lorenzo laughs.

My temper blazes when the asshole claps as if he's giving a standing ovation.

"Telling the truth is the first right thing you've ever done." His taunts slice into me deeper. "Seriously, did you really think you'd get away with grabbing some whore off the street to play your wife?"

"I'm not a whore," Megan snaps before I can answer him with a bullet to the head.

I forgot she was here. Here right next to me with Knox and Levi at her side, who look like they're ready to kill Lorenzo too.

He laughs again and shakes his head. "So what do you think you are, my dear? You were purchased for your body and your *services* at a sex club. That sounds like a fucking whore to me. You—"

I land my fist in his face and send him flying into the bookshelf. I grab my gun and I'm about to launch at him, but I'm held back by Knox and Levi.

"Fucking let me go." My voice echoes around the room.

"Cristiano, control yourself!" Grandfather yells.

"That's my girl you're talking about." I snarl at Lorenzo like a feral animal. "My wife." Rage is clouding my mind, but I know what I said, and I don't care.

The guys continue to hold me back using their full strength. If they weren't, Lorenzo would be dead now, not just looking at me with terror entrenched on his fucking face. That terror is there because I've never struck out like this before and God knows there have been enough times.

"Cristiano, stop it." Megan's meek voice is the only thing that reaches me and I feel my calm returning.

She comes up to me, tears streaming down her cheeks as she touches my arm.

"Stop. He's right. He's right, Cristiano." The desolation on her face and in her voice breaks my heart.

The guys release me when she walks out of the room and we go after her.

I catch her arm when she gets to the top of the stairs and pull her back to me.

"Baby, it's not true." I tighten my grip on her.

"What part isn't?" Tears run down her cheeks. "I became a whore when I signed my contract to work at the club. I became the whore long before the ink dried on the paper. Lorenzo is just pointing out the obvious."

"None of us care about that. I don't."

"But I do, so please just let me go." She tries to pull away, but I don't release her.

"Where are you even going?"

"Anywhere. Cristiano, we were always going to come to an end. It may as well be now. You don't need me anymore. So, just let me go."

Levi rests a hand on my shoulder and nods. "Let her go, Cristiano."

I turn to look at him and when I see the hardened expression on his face, I release her. Levi would only tell me to do something like that if he knew it was the right thing.

Megan rushes away and we watch her fly down the stairs.

"She needs to cool off. She's not going to listen to either of us when she's that upset," Knox states.

I'm about to answer when my grandfather storms out of his office and marches up to us.

"You are not to have anything to do with that girl." He raises his hand and shakes his head. "Ship her back to the States the moment she returns and cut all ties. Cross me and you can kiss the empire goodbye."

"You're seriously telling me I can't be with her?" I bare my teeth.

"You heard me loud and clear, boy."

"Then you can keep the empire because I choose her." I can't believe those words come out of my mouth, but as I hear them, they feel right.

This is a no-brainer. There was a reason I felt like I had everything when I was with Megan.

Because I did.

Grandfather looks shocked. So shocked he's not speaking. Good, because we have nothing more to say to each other and I've made my choice.

Lorenzo was right about one thing. Telling the truth was a good move.

When I walk away from my grandfather, Knox and Levi fall in step with me.

I look from one to the other, realizing I just threw away what we worked so hard to achieve.

"I'm sorry," I mutter.

"Nothing to be sorry for, friend," Knox says. "I chose her a long time ago."

"Me too," Levi concedes. "We were just waiting for you to realize you had as well."

I stare back at him, feeling more grateful than I already was for our friendship.

I almost ask them when they knew I was in love with Megan and when they knew too, but I don't. I know the answer because I can see it on their faces.

We loved her at hello.

We loved her the moment she first walked into that room with Mimi at the club and looked nervous as hell. We loved her the moment we all felt that spark and knew we couldn't be without her.

The three of us have always stuck together, but this feels different from any other time. This feels like the time that actually matters.

"We have to find a way to fix this." I speak with conviction. "That's all I want now."

"So do we."

2 0

MEGAN

Shaky legs carry me up the sweeping stone steps to Paige and James' home.

With the exception of the archways and the absence of the lake, their house would almost look like Cristiano's. The massive castle-like building looks like it was pulled from the cover of a holiday brochure designed for royalty or aristocrats.

The last time I was here, I was happy and hopeful. Paige had just gotten married and I was at grad school. We were talking about the future and all the things we wanted to do.

Paige and James are both lawyers. Law was actually how they met. James was her college professor and they had a secret affair.

After they got married, James started working on expanding his family business in Italy. Paige made me promise I'd always visit if the day came when they had to move here.

Today, my broken heart used the last ounce of strength I had left to get here.

I just hope Paige doesn't shun me and remind me that I told her to stay away from me forever. She'd have every right to do so. I've turned up on her doorstep in Italy completely unannounced.

I'm a mess and I look like shit. I couldn't get dressed properly when Cristiano woke me up to go to his grandfather's office. I also don't have anything with me like my purse.

It was one of the drivers at the house that brought me here. So I'm sure by now Cristiano knows where I am.

The same said driver had to show ID when we drove onto the property and I had to announce my presence, which means Paige and James know I'm here too.

When the guard let us through, I took that as a good sign she might be willing to talk to me, but every step I take forward feels like I've got lead attached to my feet.

I've barely rung the doorbell when the door flies open and I find myself standing face to face with Paige.

The sight of her makes my eyes water all over again. Even if this goes wrong, I'm so happy I got to see her.

As she stares at me, I think of the most important thing I need to tell her and that's how I decide to start.

"I'm so sorry, Paige," I mumble. "I'm so sorry for everything."

Before I can get another word out, she throws her arms around me.

More tears come, but this time I cry with relief.

I told Paige everything.

KHARDINE GRAY & FAITH SUMMERS

She took me out to the terrace, where we sat together, talking like old times.

I also saw James briefly before he left us to catch up.

I was so happy to see him looking at Paige the same way he always did as if he was falling deeper in love with her with every passing second.

Part of me knows I wanted love like that and my desire for it blindsided me when it came to Hunter.

As I poured out my heart and talked about all the craziness that had happened to me, she listened.

Now I'm all cried out, and I've said everything there was to say, including the fact that I'm in love with three men.

I was sure she was going to think I was crazy at that point, but I'm still waiting for her to cast judgment.

Pushing a lock of her dark hair behind her ear, she tilts her head and takes my hand.

"I'm so sorry you went through so much." She squeezes my hand and straightens. "Why didn't you call me after Hunter died? Why didn't you tell me how much trouble you were in?"

I pull in a quick breath. "I couldn't. Not after the way I treated you. I deserve what happened to me just for treating you so badly."

"Please don't say that. You were in love. I... hate what happened, but I understood because I knew how badly you wanted something good in your life. What better good could there have been than your high school sweetheart coming back to you. You thought he was the one who got away. Although I hate him, I understand where you're coming from."

I consider her reasoning and appreciate her even more. "Thank you for considering that."

"It's true, so I had to." She picks up the little blue box resting by the jug of lemonade her maid brought out. She'd gone inside to get it a few moments ago. My lips part when she holds it out to me. "This is yours."

"Mine?" I can't imagine she'd have a gift for me.

"Yes." She places the box in my hands.

"What is it?"

"All the letters I sent you over the last few months are in that box. Hunter sent them back to me. *Asshole.*"

What the actual fuck? I bring my hand to my heart and gaze back at her, utterly flabbergasted.

"You wrote to me?"

"Yes. I called and messaged too, but he got those and told me not to call you again. That was after you and I had our last argument."

And after Hunter conveniently lost my phone. That fucking asshole. I'm assuming he threw it away. My God, that man put me through so much.

"I can't believe he did that."

"I wish I could say it was love, but it couldn't have been. No one who loves you would treat you that way. I would have emailed, but I thought I'd have the same shit, so I decided to write. When he returned my letters, *opened,* I knew the only choice was to see you in person." She releases a heavy sigh. "I was meant to fly back to Chicago a few weeks ago, but I got sick."

She's smiling even though she just said she was sick.

"Sick. You look happy."

"I am because I'm pregnant."

I gasp as joy bubbles within me and I hug her. "Oh my God, Paige. This is the best news." It truly is and I'm so happy for her. "Congratulations to you and James."

When I pull away, she looks at me teary-eyed.

"Thank you. I was so worried I wouldn't get to tell you. My Mom's flying over in a few days."

"I can just imagine how happy she is."

"She cried with joy." Paige laughs, then brings her hands together. "Enough about me and enough about Hunter and the past. How about we talk about your guys."

My cheeks burn. "I know you're going to tell me I'm crazy. No one can be in love with three people. Right? It's just crazy and one of those wild things you'd hear at the club that rich people make up." Although I laugh, I sound off-key and on edge because I don't believe a word I'm saying.

Paige giggles. "If anyone was going to fall for three people, it would be you." We both laugh then the seriousness returns to her face. "And you are in love, aren't you?"

When I think of Cristiano, Knox, and Levi, I can't deny my love for them.

"Yes."

"Then it can't be crazy. It's just different. That's all it is. If different works, then who can judge you and call you crazy? I don't know how the hell you'd arrange your life with each of them, but if it works, it works."

"You're serious?"

"I am very serious. I know I got off on the wrong foot with you when it came to Hunter. I won't do that again. Not when I just got you back."

"So you forgive me?"

"Of course I do. So my first act as best friend in our newly reformed relationship is to tell you to try and sort this thing out with Cristiano, Knox, and Levi. Sounds like you have a good thing going. That's worth something."

"What about everything with Cristiano's grandfather?"

"I think that exists outside your relationship."

Is she right?

I think of everything I went through with the guys and I hope she is.

Hoping is all I can do right now because everything is a mess.

"Come on, let's get something to eat and hang out by the beach until you feel like you're ready to go back."

"I'd like that."

I stare out at the horizon as the sun sets.

I just got back to the château. After a fantastic day with Paige, I'm not sure what to expect here.

When I go into the cottage and find the guys in the living room, hope sparks my heart. Cristiano is the first to come over to me.

"I—"

"Wait. Please," he interrupts, brushing a finger over my cheek. "Before you say anything, I need to ask you what you want."

"Me?" I point to myself.

"Yes. What do you want, Megan? We know we want you because we're all in love with you, but we realize that might not be realistic or a life you want."

I stare back at him in fascination, feeling my spirits lift.

"That is what I want. You. The three of you." I look at each of them. "I love you all too. I know we haven't known each other long, but that's how I feel. All the time, we kept talking about us ending. I didn't want it to end."

"Then it doesn't have to end." Cristiano smiles and his eyes sparkle.

"But what about your grandfather? What the hell must he think of me. The truth really is that I'm a whore you got from the club. I can't change that."

"You aren't a whore. You're the woman who changed our lives." Cristiano looks back at Knox and Levi and they come up to us.

"You're the woman who made our fantasies come to life," Levi adds.

"The woman we fell for," Knox says. "And we don't care what people think of us if we're happy together."

"And I still want to marry you." Cristiano takes my hand, looking at my ring. "It makes it official that you're ours."

"Really? That's what you guys want?"

"Yes. So how about we do this?"

I look at my guys and love them harder. Cristiano, Knox, and Levi. My three knights who saved me in so many ways. I don't have to think about the answer to that question.

"Yes."

21

CRISTIANO

It's in the early hours of the morning and I'm awake again smoking. This time I'm outside the cottage, sitting on the veranda. I watched the sunrise and the day come to life.

It's still quite early and I could probably catch up on the sleep I never got last night, but I'm going to sit out here for a little longer.

We're heading back to the States in a few hours and I don't know when I'll see this side of the world again.

Once we get home, I'll have a lot of decisions to make and a lot of changes to get used to. I already spoke to my mother and told her the truth.

I wanted her to hear what was happening from me instead of my grandfather. It was my responsibility to tell her the truth anyway.

When I told her, I was glad she didn't judge me. One of the things I love about my mother is she's always been supportive no matter how bad a situation is.

Of course, she was furious about what I did, but she calmed when I told her I loved Megan and was still marrying her. It helped to hear that because she knew all the parts of my relationship I showed the world was real.

I started this journey out not wanting to get married. Now, look at me.

I know being the one to marry Megan gives me extra claim to her than Knox and Levi, but it won't be like that. We spoke at length and decided that *we* wanted to marry her. Since only one of us can do that, we agreed to stick to the original plan of me being her husband. Levi and Knox have always considered themselves as my right-hand men and that won't change even though clearly, we'll have to leave the company.

We haven't talked about that part yet other than agreeing to stick together. The world is an oyster for guys like us, so we'll have to create our own legacy.

The door opens and Megan comes out wearing her dressing gown.

I put out my cigar when she floats over to me and pull her into my lap.

"Morning. You're up early." I brush my nose over hers.

"I missed you. Are you okay?" Remorse fills her eyes. She knows we gave up the empire to be with her.

"I'm okay." I have her. If she is my everything, then I'm okay. "I don't want you to worry about anything."

"I wanted you to get the business."

"I know, but it'll be fine. Everything will be okay, baby. Don't worry about me. "I pick up a lock of her hair. "We didn't get to talk about Paige. We were busy making up."

She blushes. "It was amazing seeing her. Thanks for encouraging me to go."

"You are most welcome, wife-to-be. I love you."

She tweaks my nose playfully. "I love you too."

Our lips meet for a hungry kiss and I don't want to stop. We don't until footsteps sound on the gravel path ahead of us. When we pull apart, I'm surprised to see my grandfather standing paces away.

Megan goes rigid at the sight of him. I hope he's not going to argue with me or disrespect her. I just wanted to leave quietly and get away from here.

"Morning, sorry to interrupt you two. Can we talk, son?" His voice is much calmer than yesterday.

He also called me son. He only does that during special moments. Hearing it reminds me that I never wanted to be at war with him.

I can't be at peace either if he treats me like a child. Being the don of the family means being free from the restraints of others and having the ability to make crucial decisions on your own. He never gave me that opportunity. But out of respect, I'll hear him out.

"Sure." I look at Megan. "Baby, why don't you go inside and wait for me."

"Of course." She gets off my lap and avoids looking at my grandfather.

I stand and set my shoulders back.

"Did I hear you call her wife-to-be?" he asks.

"Yes, you did."

"You're still marrying her even after everything?"

"I am. Why are you here, Grandfather? I think we said everything that needed to be said yesterday. You aren't going to tell me what to do anymore." I'll also be damned if I'm going to let him marry Simona off to Lorenzo. "And Lorenzo isn't marrying Simona. I don't care what you say. I'm not going to allow her to suffer such a fate. I will kill his ass before you do that."

"That's why you'll make a good leader."

His words throw me and I'm not sure what to make of it. "What do you mean?"

"A good leader wouldn't be afraid to defy my authority and he wouldn't be afraid to turn down the empire for the woman he loves."

I think for a moment about what he's saying and since he seems to have seen the light, I hope this conversation goes the way I've always wanted.

"No, a good leader wouldn't be afraid of any of those things."

"That's why it should be you."

"Should it?"

"I'm not happy with what you did, Cristiano. I am hurt and disappointed you lied the way you did for something so important to me."

"I am sorry. I assure you that I am. You know your opinion matters to me more than anything, but when you insisted I got married to take over the business and even considered marrying Simona off to Lorenzo, you were out of line."

Relief floods me when he nods.

"Maybe we can fix this by forgiving each other. I'm just an old fool who wanted to see his grandson in love. And I got my wish. You looked in love just now. Although I don't understand you sharing her with Knox and Levi." His brows furrow slightly. "I guess I don't have to understand it. That's none of my business."

"We work and it makes sense," I try to explain. "There is love and that's all we need."

"Then no one can question you. I'm gathering the family

tonight, so I can hand over the business to you. I hope that you, your wife-to-be and your two capos will be there."

I smile at him and as he reaches out his hand to shake mine, I take it.

"We will."

Everything worked out and the worry is over.

I got the business, but most of all, I got the girl too.

EPILOGUE

Megan
Two years later

Salty sea breeze floats over my skin as I take a deep breath and place my hands on my ever-growing belly.

Six months ago, I got the most glorious news ever. I'm pregnant with Cristiano's son.

"Pregnancy suits you, my friend," Paige says with a laugh.

"Sometimes, I can't believe I'm pregnant. And I look like I'm ready to drop."

We both laugh and she pulls her knees to her chest, digging her toes into the sand.

We're sitting on the beach in Italy. While we've been talking, our men have been playing volleyball shirtless.

Watching them now as they battle it out reminds me of that drool-worthy scene from Top Gun where all the guys were doing the same thing. At one point in my life, I lived for that scene. Now I have my own replica.

"Are you thinking Top Gun again?" Paige giggles.

"Is it that obvious?"

"It is, but I totally get it. Three out of the four men running around shirtless belong to you."

I smile and gaze over at my guys, who look better than perfect.

As Paige's daughter, Valencia, runs past us, she catches her and pulls her into her lap. Eighteen-month-old Valencia looks exactly like her mother but has her father's eyes.

When Paige starts telling her the story of how she met me, my mind goes right back to that day.

I think of where I came from and where I am now.

I started off as the girl with a sordid past who'd lost her mother and was fighting to get her life back. It took me a while and I had to go through a lot of heartache. But I did it.

I actually did it and I know my mother would be proud. She can finally rest in peace knowing I'm okay and I made it. I got everything I ever wanted and much, much, more.

As my three princes approach me with their sexy smiles, I know my mother would also be happy I found true love.

True love with Cristiano, Knox, and Levi.

They are mine.

And I am theirs.

~

THANKS SO VERY MUCH FOR READING.
I HOPE YOU ENJOYED THIS STORY.

To dive in my Dark Odyssey world start with Tease Me Book 1 in the series.

To check out my dark mafia world start with Ruthless Prince, the first book in the Dark Syndicate series.

ACKNOWLEDGMENTS

For my readers.
Always for you.
Thank you for reading my stories.
I hope you continue to enjoy my wild adventures xx

ABOUT THE AUTHOR

Faith Summers is the Dark Contemporary Romance pen name of USA Today Bestselling Author, Khardine Gray. Warning !! Expect wild romance stories of the scorching hot variety and deliciously dark romance with the kind of alpha male bad boys best reserved for your fantasies.
Dive in and enjoy her naughty page-turners.

Made in the USA
Columbia, SC
30 October 2022